The
LAST
to DIE

William Herrick

SECOND CHANCE PRESS
Sag Harbor, N.Y. 11963

Copyright © 1971 by William Herrick
Originally published by Simon and Schuster

First republication 1984 by
SECOND CHANCE PRESS
RD2, Sag Harbor, New York

Library of Congress Catalogue Card Number: 83-051507
ISBN: 0-933256-47-7 (cloth)
　　　0-933256-48-5 (paper)

PRINTED IN THE UNITED STATES OF AMERICA

FOR NATALIE

". . . we live at a time when man believes himself fabulously capable of creation, but he does not know what to create. Lord of all things, he is not lord of himself."

ORTEGA Y GASSET

I

The curious eye of the soldier observed him through a crack in the batten door. The captive sat calmly at the wooden table before the open notebook that had been given him at his request, the ballpoint pen held lightly in his slender fingers. When interrogated, the captive had shrugged, refused to answer any questions, even as to his name, and then had asked for paper and pen.

"No matter what I say, it will be misunderstood," the man had said quietly, softly, in total command. "Let me write it down so at least I'll be misunderstood in my own words, over my own signature." Abruptly the man had laughed, his large white teeth gleaming in the handsome tanned face. His laugh had been merry enough but had continued a bit too long, for it concluded with a bad cough, and then a fleck of blood bubbled at the corner of his mouth.

So they had given him the paper and pen, had bolted the door, and left. Now the man sat ever so calmly thinking long over what to write, or at least how to begin. Yet, strangely, every once in a while the captive would cock an ear as if he heard something in the distance, or was listening for a word, a sound, a voice. The soldier wondered about it but gave it little time. The hut was surrounded with armed soldiers, their carbines on the ready. Perhaps the captive was listening for the footsteps which would ultimately fall and would sound his end.

Still the soldier's dark, curious eye observed the caged man. He saw him bite his lower lip, smile to himself, and raise his shoulders almost imperceptibly in that way people have of indicating it matters little what they say or do not say, but they will say it anyway, like it or not, what the hell, the world won't come to an end.

The man leaned over his notebook, lowered his pen, began to write, paused, cocked an ear in that strange fashion, resumed. The soldier hunched his shoulders, sat on the earthen floor, his carbine between his legs, his back against the bolted door.

II

Having made my decision, I no longer hesitate. There are after all no laws—legal or extra—that dictate where I must begin. If there are, it does not matter. I have lived outside the law, and now that time is at an end, there is none that can reach me. As always, I do as I please, or more accurately, as I am compelled to do.

Strange . . . as I touch pen to paper, I can hear their horses behind me, still outdistanced, in a slow canter along the disused railroad pass that leads from the unworked mine. They will, I am certain, call jeeps to the pursuit, but that will take them some time. I decide to work my way into the mountains and cross the border. Fortunately border patrols are rare in this part of the world. No one cares.

I enter a stand of black walnut and mahogany at an old cut, an ancient, now overgrown, logging road. It winds upward. The thaw is on and the runoff underfoot flows swiftly. It will roil into the culvert—a hollowed tree trunk—this side of the narrow dirt road and empty with a quick seething rush into the underbrush a good fifty feet above the bog, then push downward through a heavy growth of wild grape vines, red sumac, and jacaranda into the creek. This is the same creek from which I and my band obtained our water when we came this way two months ago, twenty men and three women equipped with excellent submachine guns, ample ammunition strapped over the backs of several fat little donkeys and sturdy pack horses, positive that victory would be ours. Yesterday the remainder of my band were killed or taken captive. Only I remain free.

Unless my pursuers turn off at the dirt road bridge, they will miss my tracks and proceed to the end of the pass, formerly a gravel pit. I will by then have crossed over the crest of the lower mountains and gained a few hours. Enough time to win. Win? Only one victory remains for me now. A victory to reward the worms.

As I proceed upward, the last snow still holds off the sun with a thin shell of ice that makes sudden shifts and cracks. Mountain otter and deer tracks are disappearing in the melt. I rest, my back against a young, still slender, mahogany. My lungs ache, my fingers quiver, my lips are drained of blood. I am too old for running— stamina gone, tire too quickly. No, it isn't that at all; I am begging for alms. I am in excellent condition; it is the altitude. Seven, eight thousand feet. On the plateau it will be worse. Altitude there is well over ten thousand, and the ichu grass.

When I tire I begin to cough, to spit blood, the residue of an infantile illness. On the puna, the plateau, the red of my blood will glisten on the ichu grass under the tropical sun, just as the blood of Buteo glistened on the slag of the old mine after the assault. My illness is eccentric. During the two months of the campaign it never betrayed me. It was the comradeship which purified my lungs. Now that I am alone it will again begin its rot, as it always has in the past. As it rotted in the capital of the peninsula after power had been seized and the integrity of the old band began its disintegration under the hammering of the conflict for personal enhancement. I refused to be either the hammer or the anvil—each, to me, an indignity. Again I was the foreigner, neither the servant nor the master. I suffer from the ancient illness: I must be I.

I cough and I bleed.

As I did in the days of my pubescent youth in the house of my old ones, of my brothers and sisters, among whom I was the youngest. The house is large, spacious, with many sun-washed rooms, dormered, painted white, the floors polished gold acacia, its whorls a choreography for many dancers, across which servants moved lightly, quietly, on felt slippers. From my window I could see the pastures, the meadows, the wooded hills, and far in the distance the jagged outline of the mountains, a singular graph on the perimeter of the vast sky. The barns stood low, rambling, freshly painted black, opening into a fenced paddock in which the mares with foal lazed, indifferent to the angry stallions gnawing on the heavy-timbered barrier between them.

Once, when I was twelve, I saw a stallion rise high on his hind legs, buck, majestically leap the barrier, scatter the mares wildly, drive one to the fence, rise mightily to mount her. Gracefully she reared, pirouetted on slender ankles. Both on hind legs, gently they touched hoof to hoof and muzzle to muzzle. Again on all fours, they resumed the dance, faster and faster, but the stallion's frenzy availed him nothing. I laughed with excitement,

13

threw the window open and urged the stallion on. "Take her! Take her!"

My father, now standing at my side, said quietly, "No, Ramón, he is a beast. Only man can rape." I coughed and I bled.

I miss the old ones, haughty but loving . . . yet never understanding. I concluded my education, said my farewells to parents, siblings, home and country. Disappeared. Vanished like steam into air. To rise like the wisps of a ghostly fog from the blue glacial waters of Lake Prespa in the northwest corner of Greece where I found comradeship for a time with Markos and his guerrillas against an idiot throne. There in the mountains, the cough stopped, and the bleeding. Healed by the hardships, the deprivation, the fighting. A flaming fraternity burned to ash.

I press hard with my back against the mahogany, my eyes intent on the dirt bridge, the jacaranda, my ears open only to the slow canter of their horses. I grasp the stock of my gun more firmly. It is a fine weapon, sturdy, rapid, lethal. Suddenly I miss my binoculars, lost among the debris of the mine. Still the sun, yet low in the east, will silhouette the army patrol as it emerges into the open of the bridge. It hardly matters. Die now or later, what difference? Habit. Habit now more than will.

By will, and habit too, I inform my respiratory system to slow its pace. Save your breath. My eyes are locked on the huge jacaranda tree, still bare, spring buds hard and blue, that marks the bridge.

Abruptly the sound of hooves has ceased. And for a moment my breathing as well. Yes, they are walking their horses. Only a man can expend his life running. Horses must have their rest.

I wait.

Listen.

Hear the wind blowing on the trees, the raucous cry of tropical birds as they sail high above the valley, the hum of a host of insects among the brush, the throbbing of my heart, the drumming in my head. Where are they? Even walking their horses they should by now have approached the bridge. If Buteo were with me, we would have prepared the bridge for them. Made them welcome with an explosive salute. *Their* blood would have glistened in the sun, men and horses disemboweled. Even the jacaranda would have been moved. But a man alone can only run, obsessed with his fear and his pursuers.

Have they turned off, taken some trail to the plateau above me, decided to come at me from behind?

Panic intrudes wildly and I impress my spine on the hard mahogany, hug my gun to myself, as if begging both the tree's and the gun's calm indifference to make me so. I feel the presence of an eye, saurian, probing into the back of my bristling neck. With a spastic lurch I leap to my feet, search about. Nothing. "You're scaring, and at the very beginning too," I say aloud. "Either catch hold or pound a bullet into your head. Remember who you are. A million posters on a million walls. CORDES!"

I grip the stock of my submachine gun, a Russian make, most efficient. "This gun in competent hands can incapacitate more men in one minute than you can count. Treat it kindly and it will reciprocate." They always smiled when I told them that. "Or, to put it another way, a hammer in a skilled artisan's hand will never bend the nail, only drive it home." I thrust my fist at them in the old Roman style and they laughed.

And *I* laugh now in memory of our fraternity and it brings down upon me a sudden thunderclap, a crashing of brush, a sharp retort like a snapping tree. I swing about, the stock of the gun digging a hole in my chest. In time to see a huge condor take flight. Its wingspread casts a shadow as ominous as that of a fighter plane. Before I can slow my breathing, I see the eye staring at me. Coldly, calmly, lazily. From the ugly head of a sloth as it hangs from the branch right above me.

Quivering with revulsion, I retreat from the tree and open a flask I carry in my rucksack and quaff the last of the Mexican tequila, my favorite drink, derived from mescal. A wild fire, it lays waste to my fear.

I am behaving like a frightened child, as if I had never before known danger, been at arm's length with death. Why, just yesterday, at the mine, after I led my band into the trap—set by whom?—I maintained my calm and almost extricated them with the loss of but a few men, for it is at that moment, when life is most precarious in the great confraternity which is an intensely fought battle, that I feel I am most alive. It is when I am alone that I become fearful, easily frightened, skittish at every sound, every breath, certain the shadow of every tree conceals an enemy. Either solely alone or alone in a crowd. What enemy? And why precisely in a time of utter solitude? Simply because it is during those moments I must constantly ask myself what is the single way that I must go? Driven, impelled, an impatient bullet couched in the steel chamber awaiting the finger's twitch.

My eyes intent on the bridge and the railroad pass, I am like a cat who eats, relieves himself, licks his asshole and yet is never unaware that the dog is around the corner.

16

If the patrol has gone to the plateau above me I will hear every twig in its path snap a good mile away. They would know that, since they know the cuts, passes, footbridges to the plateau and even to the mountain peaks beyond better than I. Without Buteo to guide me, even with the maps I have, I am in a maze. Marguerite has snipped the twine and rolled in her end. And Buteo lies dead back there, an impatient bullet having traversed its single way. Stolid, earnest Buteo had come from this very land to fight alongside me in the mountains of the peninsula, and had guarded over me like a duenna. To preserve my life for the revolution. That slow, sturdy man with the quick hands who used his rifle like a spray gun, the enemy so many flies.

"Christ, you're cruel, Buteo," someone had said. "What are you going to be like after we win?"

He had blanched, lowered his eyes, remained dumb for a few moments, words formed with difficulty. Then he had smiled sadly. "Yes, we are a cruel people. Are we to endure cruel lives and remain tender? Loving? Merciful?" Abruptly he turned and walked away.

Afraid to say what it would be like after. We were all afraid.

Yet Buteo had loved his land and his people with a delicate tenderness and a graceful mercy. We are men, therefore we live in contradiction. Forgive us. Be merciful and tender. Beneficent. He came from the direst poverty, his parents, his kind, all serfs. For this tropical inland paradise of alluvial plains, fertile forests and snow-capped peaks, each within clear vision of the other, equatorial to arctic, Indian, mestizo, white, some four or five million, is ruled by several barons, and no king. Perhaps that is why I had chosen this land in which to make my revolution. And Buteo would be

17

king. Buteo had smiled when the decision was made. "When you see the peaks of our mountains you will know those of the peninsula are as small as your Marguerite's breasts." Ha. How true.

I am wandering, my concentration is without compass. I am here alone, without Buteo, without a reconnaissance patrol, without lookouts, without my band. The professional has suddenly become an amateur. That is my great problem now. An agitated imagination, a reliance on intuition, a paucity of knowledge all bar professionalism. I adjure that face to face with the enemy I will again be the professional. Of that I must be certain or I cannot go on. A lifetime of some four decades will otherwise have been wasted. A man is as he finds himself at his moment of death. How cruel.

I clasp the gun with confidence. I will follow the sun, my eyes always on the highest peaks, and I will know my heading is west. Once I cross the border I will know my way. They will not dare to follow me—will not risk an international incident. Not for an unknown man. Rojos may well have betrayed me, his rationale that my romanticism was destroying the orthodox revolution, but he would not have let it be known that Ramón Cordes led the guerrilla band. He, they, acknowledge it serves the revolution—any revolution—that I remain a mystery. A grand joke on the enemy. Invisible, I am the spectre of revolution which haunts them—frightens them. Invisible, it can be asserted I am at Nanterre, Berlin, Detroit, Rio de Janeiro. Invisible, I am a wandering revolutionary in the way there were once wandering minstrels, playing my electric lute. And the children dance.

But my alleged friends must be blind as well. For if I am at Berkeley, then I am also in Prague, in Shanghai,

18

in Havana. The contradictions fly. They soar. Red Rosa's skirts can be heard to rustle in Warsaw and Federica's on Las Ramblas.

And I? When I sat behind a desk on the peninsula, performing my daily tasks listlessly—how I abhor specifics—I was just that: a man sitting behind a desk. Uneasily. I disappeared. Some said I had been executed by my loyal friend who ruled. Others swore they had seen me in Algiers, in Peking, on the sidewalk of Les Deux Magots conferring with Him and Her, an unlikely ménage. It has, of course, been rumored that Ramón Cordes leads the guerrillas in Buteo's land. Still others have asked, But why? He does not speak the tongue of the countryside, he has little knowledge of the economy, none of its history. He may be incorrigibly romantic, but he is also a professional revolutionary, it is hardly likely he would have crossed the line into sanity. Indeed!

They asked questions which I refused to answer.

So here I am, but to the enemy I might very well be elsewhere. They will not follow me across the border, and with an extra hour or two I will make my escape.

I turn my eyes away for a moment from the bridge, the tall jacaranda, to examine the sloth. Still there upsidedown, its saurian eye contemptuous. I should kill it with my knife for no reason but to indicate my lack of fear. I will plunge my knife into the ugly little beast and its blood will spurt like Moby Dick's spout, and I will observe it coldly as it bleeds to death with a gush. I begin to rise, deciding on the spur of pleasure to perform the deed—but no! Hooves hammer on the bridge planking, saddles groan, and I turn swiftly, teeth on edge, revenge forgotten.

There they are! Five, one a commander. They stand

19

high in the saddle, horses reined, carbine barrels brilliant in the morning sun. Rapidly I calculate the odds, raise my gun, its stock angry against my chest. No, Ramón. If another man were with me, Buteo, an excellent rifleman, the odds would be in our favor. Surprise, et cetera. These guns are very good. But alone I do not dare. I am not quite as romantic as friends and enemy have said. About this matter of killing I am very professional. One measures chances, gambles only when the odds are favorable.

They are speaking, obviously deciding what direction to follow. Suddenly I am heartened. By their gestures I can see they are speaking of splitting, three to go along the railroad pass, two to follow the cut I have taken. If that is the course they choose, I will follow the two and kill them. If the three then overtake me, I could with this gun as opposed to their carbines, in addition to the tactical advantage, kill them as well. At least the odds would be most favorable.

They are uncertain. They discuss it further. I sit quietly, observing them from the distance, as above me that slothful eye slowly drills a hole into the back of my neck. I become impatient, my mouth is dry, I dare not move, my breath bellows with difficulty, but fear is eager to spring forward. They are deciding my fate and I am helpless, totally without control, fearful for a man who must always have control, mastery over his every move. I begin to feel claustrophobic, chained, gagged, in one of those vertical cells where it is impossible to sit or lie down, merely able to stand or lean, and my lungs seem to be shut off and I think I will suffocate. I force myself to raise the gun, I will take the risk, thus controlling my own fate, deciding for myself when I shall die.

They have decided. No, they will not divide themselves, they are clever enough, know the weapon I carry. It had been for me merely a hope, which I daresay means I still run with life. They have assumed, I am certain—a certainty derived from an intuitive source—that I will have decided on the fastest route, up the railroad pass. And the wisest, for they are following the assumption that I am I, a foreigner to this land, unfamiliar with the maze of passes through the mountain. From the end of the railroad, the gravel pit, I could then take the road that leads to the highway, that, again, leads through farm and pasture lands, and there I could hope to find a friendly peasant or shepherd to conceal me until a vehicle were obtained to take me to the capital. In the capital, Rojos or Marguerite, like it or not, would have to hide me until means could be found to smuggle me from the country.

The soldiers and their captain—his gold braid glints in the sun filtering through the jacaranda boughs—are professionals, too, accustomed to reasoning coldly, weighing chances, permitting logic to lead step by step to conclusion. They plan ahead. If the prey is who they hope it is, the rewards will be magnificent. In every capital of the world, east and west, the stone-assed will dance. The spectre is dead. An anomaly. How does one drill a spectre with holes? Burn him at the stake? Hang him? No matter, they will not concern themselves with that. On the peninsula, of course, my loyal friend will not dance, merely wrap a contemptuous smile round a fat cigar. For twenty-four hours no one will find it necessary to tell him how fantastic, fabulous, formidable he is. Almighty. He might even permit himself silence for thirty minutes. But from the silence will rise a eulogy so verbose archaeologists will have to dig through the words for a thousand years to get at my bones.

Not yet. Have patience, loyal friend.

No, not yet. My pursuers plan ahead logically. They are orderly. And that is all to my advantage. Because I understand them, as they do not understand me. I am vagarious, emotional, dwell in chaos, yet, like a split atom, I am contained in a lead and steel casing. Target: the world.

Still, at this moment, there is an inevitable logic. They must pursue me, and I must be pursued.

I shrug. Smile bitterly. The five horsemen have indeed crossed the bridge and are cantering along the railroad pass. A good clear run. I myself turn and slowly begin to ascend the winding cut which leads from the cabecera del valle to the plateau.

I have won an hour.

III

Their broad, soldierly backs invite my
bullets. Impulsively I raise the gun. No. I refuse. Not
from sentimentality, which I can ill afford, but from discipline, my sole remaining wealth. Now, screened from
view by the foliage lining the pass, I am seized by indecision. I have erred. Chances be damned, I should have
emptied my clip! Two or three would have fallen, been
killed, wounded—unfortunately, not every bullet kills—
and perhaps several of their horses. And they should, I
argue, at this very moment know your exact position.
The shots would have been heard miles away; reinforce-
ments rushed by jeep, by horse. The result would have
been an hour lost, not won, and they would have surrounded you, covered every path to the plateau. Self-
indulgence and bravado are for children, not for those
who wish to rule, to survive. Time has been won. Move
on!

I do not budge. The tree trunk supports my back. My
head droops, my mind wanders. Buteo is sprawled on
the slag, his swift hands emptying clip after clip in a
dense, fanlike fire at the enemy. He ignores the death so

23

sullenly, so grotesquely heaped about him. The massive fire of the enemy soldiers converges on his exposed presence and he is nailed to the slag, his legs and arms flapping wildly like a huge butterfly being frantically stabbed by a cruel child. His eye finds mine, abrasive, staring, stone.

I could have saved Buteo, that I know. The moment, the place, the circumstance had merged perfectly for one judicious word that would have preserved his dignity and not injured mine. A lost moment; an unspoken word. And Buteo is dead, his crudely chiseled countenance smashed to dust. Self-indulgent vanity had thrust him forward, envy had stopped my tongue, yet it is less difficult to assert that history had ordered his death. Less difficult because it stays the tears. Tears corrode the will. Will supine, fear sports like a wild dog.

Marguerite.

She is a slender, sweeping, graceful line drawing of a woman, with the pointed head of a doe, and large, burning, promising eyes. It is the promise of those eyes, the obvious stance and clothes, a mite too carefully draped, too uniquely chic perhaps, which lead all men who encounter her to believe she is without underthings and prepared at a glance to be led by the hand under the stairs.

A charade. She is a self-manufactured article, a mannequin modeled after the sultry cinema stars of the twenties, the tourists' demimondaines of the Latin Quarter, the picture postcards sold in Oriental bazaars. Naked she is nothing, merely a linkage of slender bones fleshed sparely, leanly, ass scrawny, breasts sorrowfully delinquent, a wiry black crop. A desolation. Entering

24

her is as frustrating as having a monumental itch in the small of the back and finding no wall on which to scratch. She huffs and puffs, moans and groans, pyramiding to what you are certain will be the apocalypse. Universe destroyed, rebirth.

A false pregnancy. Nothing!

Stop, Cordes, your cruelty reveals your hatred.

Who made the promises she could not keep? Etched, sculpted, painted, emblazoned—all larger than life?

No, no, Cordes, cruelty once launched must proceed full steam ahead. Give it vent. Let it go. Vile half-woman afraid to be whole.

Gifted by birth with a superior intelligence, she devotes most of it to developing cunning ploys simultaneously to inform you of *her* virtues and talents and *your* deficiencies. For recompense—she wishes to diminish you, yet retain your love—she lavishes praise so profusely you are soon embarrassingly aware it is false. Full of praise, still, with the smug arrogance of the deeply neurotic and the glutted meanness of a narrow soul, she informs you your virtues are of the uninteresting breed: you are mature, responsible, steady, unneurotic. What a bore. She of course, said with a smug little smile, indigo-painted lids lowered to conceal the eyes, is neurotic, erotic, temperamental, irresponsible, uninhibited, free.

In truth, she is a truant bourgeoise. A nasty little soul.

She has learned from her own truth that she is evil, envious, venomous, but, unhappy with the world's frowns—hypocrites!—she has constructed a façade of goodness for herself. Jerry-built. The slightest tremor and it splinters with a whine at your feet. She smiles sweetly, commiseratingly, speaks softly, intimately, asking after your welfare, only to warehouse every secret with which you inform her to patronize and demean you. You soon learn when she accuses you of falseness that she has just lied; of betrayal, that she has been guilty of treachery; when she cries, "Why do you hate me?", that she is filled with hatred. Every defect, foible, evil she possesses she lays on your back. And by the time she is through with you—at the precise moment she sees herself fully revealed in your eyes—she is absolutely right. Then she moves on with her little disease and you (and those around you) must suffer yours until you manage somehow to cure yourself.

All form and no substance, poor girl. Arid, stony desert—enough, Cordes, enough! You're gnawing on the bones.

Still I do not move, the tree my spine. A strange lassitude invades me. Dry-eyed, my head begins to nod, my lids to close.

It frightens me and I leap to my feet, raise the flask to suck out the tequila dregs, bitter mescal. Head tilted, sucking, I am ensnared by the eye of the sloth. It is he who has infected me. I lose no time. Draw my knife, lash it to the barrel of my gun, with a deliberate fury puncture the beast at the throat and slash him his length to his tail. Blood pours from this visceral mouth until he is dead. I stand astonished at the volume of blood the fat little body has stored. Dead, he still clings with his obscene tiny feet to the bough, his saurian eye open. His blood, I note as I wipe my knife clean on my trouser leg, is as red as mine.

I do not belabor this observation since I make it only to help me hold on to reality. In solitude one needs those

26

little things. I urinate, and it is a simple reminder that I am a chemical laboratory. I think, feel, therefore I am palpable, alive, real. Then why do I run? That is unreal. I was born to conflict, have been defeated, and now it is either run or die. I do not wish to die. A simple statement, yet proof that I have not yet exhausted the conflict. Victory is still possible.

March, Cordes, march!

Rucksack on back, gun in hand, knife in sheath, I ascend the old logging road toward the puna, the plateau. The lassitude has vanished, the burden on my back has squared my shoulders, the bloodletting cleared my brain, the higher altitude, the lighter air have begun to intoxicate me.

In command, I order, "March!" Like a good soldier, I do. Left, right, left, right. The world stands still for me. The wind is calm. The leaves do not rustle. The limbs of the trees on either side of the logging road intertwine above me in an arboreal clasp of hands, like lovers or young friends. The sun filters through the young buds and spring leaves and there is a mingling of soft, lyrical colors in a delicate wash on the remaining snow, itself slowly disappearing into the earth. The trills of the birds are sweet with a discordant melody. My solitude has been acknowledged by the forest and its life, for on one side I see a rare spectacled bear emerge from between two black walnut trees, peer at me without suspicion through his black-rimmed eyes, nod, and trundle off. I wave after him with a smile, knowing for once that this time my gesture of friendship won't be transformed into a gesture of self-destruction. The phrase is from the Pole, Hlasko. He also said he could not bear the idea

27

that what he'd said might hurt anyone. Did he mean only the innocent? May we say nothing to hurt the cruel? I do not wish to think about it for I can feel a cough in my chest tensing for a leap to my throat.

I resume my solitude, my oneness with the forest, its life, its melody. These are my roots, I am a native at last.

For I am a man of no national characteristics, no love of country, no attachment to family, virtues which by their nature should have made me into a great international revolutionary. The nation state is dead. Et cetera. Instead these virtues became my most profound weaknesses. Not only have I been called old-fashioned, but— and I do not know which is worse—a foreigner. On the peninsula I was loved, admired, revered by the people— or at least so I was told—but when power was won, and not until that point, I was made to understand I was an alien. A beloved alien. "He is not one of ours." I am not bitter. That has been my choice. I am not constructed for the seat of power, my ass is much too lean for that. I prefer a canvas tent or leanto under the trees, my guerrilla band, and danger from the unseen enemy.

It is not that I am alienated, nothing as mindless as that, as self-pitying—or as arrogant—it is that I have no patience with specifics, they are too hard, too sharp and crass for me. Not because I feel myself too superior, too Olympian for specifics—that is, I admit, so—but also because I cannot concentrate on lists, data, figures. I slide into generalizations, the world view; though obsessed with my own point of view, I can, at least interiorly, comprehend the other's, even have sympathy for it. Adequate proof that within me dwells a counterrevolutionary. I look around to ascertain that there are no snoopers about from the Left Bank.

I am here. I am totally alone. The trees merely sing, do not speak, do not listen. The sun is mute. The snow melts and cracks. The beasts and serpents lodged in the forest dance their inevitable pas de deux. Prey on prey. So the earth was made. And man? A beastly savage who dreams. We reach out hopefully, tenderly, for truths like slippery fingers; once grasped, they reveal themselves to be both pitiless and unconsoling.

What is my truth? My dream?

A dream constructed from fantasies derived from intangible hopes. I did not always seek death. That is a recent phenomenon, come upon me with the stealth of spiders, the silent industriousness of ants.

Wait! What is that? I hear movement, the whisper of blades of grass, the breath of phantasmagoria, the slither of a hundred snakes, the sighing of snails.

Have they come upon me?

My body trembles, yet I clasp the gun with firmness. Because my fear is great does not mean I will yield easily. I wait. No, it is not fantasy. There is a quivering among the trees—there! among the cedars, the heavy limbs sway. I hold my ground, the gun ready. It is the invisibility that frightens me. No sooner than I see his eyes shall I become strong. Eye to eye the enemy is palpable. One kills him.

"Come forward!" I say.

Silence.

Again the breath, the whisper, the sigh. I am hypnotized by the sibilance. It insinuates itself into my very pores, issuing its poison.

A leaf flutters. Involuntarily I yield a step, press the trigger of my gun. The air explodes. Birds screech and scream. The explosion reverberates among the trees and they tremble. The echoes pyramid until they escape the heights of the forest and lose themselves in the sky for a long moment, only to make one last hollow call as they career off a rocky mountainside.

Silence.

My eyes are intent on the cedars. Whoever it is has received a burst of ten without a sound. But the cedars tremble.

Now I am petrified—for his flat, pointed head begins slowly to rise from the grasses, his eyes, black pearls, intent upon me. It is the eyes that can drive a man mad. It is the eyes that make a man, a beast, alive. It is the eyes that reveal the inner pain, the betrayal. Life's contemptuous laugh. No, you are not immortal. Eyes, eyes, plastered on the walls of the world. Buteo's eyes.

The flat head rises on a thick, muscular neck. Rises and rises until it is half the height of a tree. It is a gigantic anaconda. A huge gullet. The plump outlines of some beast he had just recently swallowed throbs like an aching goiter five feet below his sleek, evil head.

His eyes never leave mine. Majestic, commanding, impenetrable, he holds me captive. He stands there vertically a good ten, twelve feet above me, the other half of him coiled among the grasses and cedars, two rows of gleaming ebony diamonds ornamenting his back. Slowly he opens his narrow jaws and flicks his burning red slimy tongue. Then like a tough black elm bending in a storm he arches toward me, a gigantic muscular arm, to encircle me, his regal black eyes never leaving mine.

No fantasy, real, a living creature, he innocently opposes my lethal, man-made weapon. I fire and cut him in two with a burst.

A tremendous electric spasm, a thrashing farewell, he

30

dies. From the upper half of the huge gullet a plump forest rat slides free. It gasps for breath, wobbles slowly to its feet, escapes into the underbrush.

I marvel.

The liberator laughs.

IV

I have succeeded to the puna, to the ichu grass, as my pursuers must by now have succeeded to the gravel pit. It will open like a huge maw and devour them, horses, guns, and all. And I will be free. I will dance among the vicuña and alpaca; the shepherds shall be my friends. I shall become one of them. Tend my flocks for eternity. Bread and cheese shall be my fare, an Indian maiden my wife, children my joy.

The dream revives me. My step is firm, yet light. The high sun warms my face. Flask empty, I drink from my canteen, and the icy water ravishes the still quivering tendrils of my fear.

For a few moments peace is mine. Why not? Have I not earned it? For good or ill, everything I have ever done since leaving the security of my familial wealth has been done to right the wrong of our great riches as opposed to the poverty of the many, to rid the world of conquerors and conquered, of victors and victims. Has it been my fault that in the wake of my successes other victors and victims have followed? It seems the world is peopled with men, when for revolutions saints are required.

Still, I carried on with the hope that the final, complete victory would put an end to that savage game. Unlike Chateaubriand, I saw the first head carried on the end of a pike, and I did not recoil. Only the weak recoil, I said, and sauntered forth to spike a head for myself to prove that I, too, was strong. I wagged his head like a banner, his wispy hair like streamers in the wind, his dripping blood like an overly sweet wine. Soon everyone reassumed his rightful place—the caudillo, the sycophants, the courtiers, the jesters, the ever-hopeful masses, and the atomized defeated lumpen.

Still, I repeat, I have earned this moment of peace. To think otherwise is to admit the futility of my existence for twenty years. A hundred.

I bask in my tranquil dream.

The puna is vast, a plain of sinuous grass gleaming in the sun; unbroken. Far below to the east is the lush tropical valley marked by serpentine rivers; standing high above to the west are the peaks with their tight caps of virgin snow. It is as if the puna were the palms of God's hands and the peaks his outstretched fingers, gnarled, calloused, thick-knuckled, broken-nailed, clutching at what even to him is an elusive heaven in order to escape the magnetism of the earth. For him, too, a hopeless gesture.

I peer into the heights, and again I laugh. Your torment is permanent, eternal; mine at least short-lived. That is how we repay you, oh, Comrade: we co-opt you to our cause.

I find a brook, a runoff from the mountains, cut deeply into the plateau, alive, sprightly, in a hurry to drop to the valley to nourish its earth.

Since I am profligate, I decide to waste a quarter of

the hour I have won. Lay my gun, rucksack aside. Shed my jumpsuit—of my own design for guerrilla use. Pockets on the outer thighs, inner thighs, along the sleeves, on the chest, over the buttocks, camouflage green. It has been reproduced and sold throughout the world together with my guerrilla code book, a tie-in sale. Buy it, the code book, a gun, and you also can be a guerrilla.

I undress. Except for my hands below the wrists and my head, which are sun-blackened, my body is white. Forty years old, I am still lean, muscular, graceful. I eat sparely and keep active. Fat guerrillas die fast. I withdraw a cake of brown soap from my rucksack—clean guerrillas don't rot—and bathe in the icy mountain waters until I am rose-red. Splash about. Never having learned, I cannot swim. Or fly. Cordes is an earthling.

Gasping, breathless, I make an exhilarating escape from the melted snow and scamper about, the ichu grass whipping my legs, my dripping behind, my frolicking pistolet. Oh, for an Indian maiden to give me surcease, comfort. After Marguerite, her solid flesh and broad hips would give my frolicker reason once again to lift his head with the knowledge that the world isn't all desert and stone, that there are soft hills and fertile gardens. He will dance and leap and somersault on the soft plains of her belly, and I will sleep with my head couched on her substance.

Oh, my Marguerite, am I being unfair? I have so little time. Caught unawares, in your suddenly revealed innocence, you have all the mysteries in your dark face, all the darkness I have ever sought in the corners of a room in shadow, a foreboding, a chronic search for a lost exquisite pain buried deep beyond all reach, the grace of the forest, the gentle touch of a bird alighting on its nest, the momentary angry wildness until the young are found hiding under the leaves, the passion that belongs to those who live with some unannounced fear so it is like a wail and a gasp. Full of promise to all men, their reach, their hope, their dreams, you have yielded to none. You are like me, Marguerite, lost in the wilds, for whom life is war and death peace.

Marguerite is a revolutionary, a native of this country, her father a prominent physician in the capital, her mother heiress to unsurpassed wealth. She is received in the highest society, where she smiles graciously at the ladies and dazzlingly at their husbands. She weaves her way daringly among them, loyal to no one but Rojos, a power waiting patiently in the wings to make his trumpeting entry to the stage center of history. Rojos counts her among his superior agents.

I count her as my executioner. But it was I who calmly placed my neck and head upon the cutting block.

That is why I am here, though for the moment I have forgotten . . . the brook, the ichu grass, the peaks like gnarled fingers, tips white with frost, and below the valley half-hidden by a dense, floating mist disintegrating at edges shot with blue-green. The sun has dried me. I dress, find a bush to shade me from the sun, munch on sour crackers, goat cheese, drink cool water from my canteen. Yearn for a sour wine or mordant tequila, smoke half a cigar instead, a Havana, from the box Marguerite had brought us just two days before. Brought in the little red Lancia to the Portal from whence she had been led on horse by Armas to our camp in the valley. I smoke and I drowse, my gun close at hand. Soon I must resume my way. The horsemen having left the gravel pit are, I am certain, at this very moment inquiring along the highway. Receiving negative response, they will think either I have obtained help or I have gone the way I have and will telegraph ahead to their commanders to have me cut off. Still I doubt they will. It will be admission on their part that, having had me, they have lost me. If their commanders are like me they will have their heads.

I strap my rucksack shut, check my gun, am about to rise when I hear a horse neigh close at hand. I repress a cry, fall back swiftly, stealthily, melt into the bush, wait. The horse's hooves are so close I can hear the long grass rustle against its flanks, can see the booted leg in the stirrup, the scabbarded carbine, can smell the rich aroma of horse sweat and leather, feel the sting of the swishing tail. My gun points its sightless yet unerring eye; the bullet attends patiently. It is a soldier and he is so close I can kill him before he will be aware that a moment has passed. The advantage, of course, is mine. The urge is great, presses upon me anxiously, but I dare not since where there is one soldier there must be more; he is most probably an advance lookout. His back is broad in the saddle, his shirt purple from sweat. He reins in the horse at the brook, dismounts. One leg is shorter than the other and he wears a built-up boot, still he moves with ease, without caution. I wonder, is he alone? He permits the horse to drink, he himself smokes a cigarette, drinks from his canteen. He removes his cap, his hair is black, wet, plastered to his large head, and he wipes the perspiration from his neck. Yes, apparently alone. No horsemen follow.

He prepares to remount his horse, has a foot in the stirrup, changes his mind. Stares about, and I cringe behind the bush. I hate to cringe. It demeans me. Life or death, it filthies me. To cringe in fear, to hide from death, is demeaning beyond words. That scum makes *me* cringe? Put an end to him. The man's a toad—a soldier for the rich. Steady pay, beans and meat. An armed servant. How the servants bowed and scraped in my father's house. Gave the young their teats to suck. Slept with the master and the master's sons. Shoulders bowed, back humped, feet in felt slippers to creep about quietly to do their work as the masters slept. Shoveled the dung, scoured the barns, burned the garbage. Degraded.

Shoot him! He is alone. The horse will be yours. He sighs. With stub finger wipes sweat round loosened collar. Peers into the distance. Duty calls. The master beckons. The brook woos him as it had me. Sighs again. The sun scorches. No! He will rebel. Begins to undress.

He is short, broadbacked, thick-necked, and without the built-up boot, gimp-legged. Hops about. Swart, apparently an Indian, perhaps a mestizo. Muscles coil about his legs, thighs, arms; his back and shoulders are padded with muscle. Step, hop, step, hop—it is like a dance to discordant music. Webern. Stravinsky. Hops, leaps into the brook with a loud breathy gasp, splashes about the freezing water, laughs as though tickled. "Br-r-r-r. Aaah!" The horse ignores him, nibbling greedily on the grass, a bay mare with spindly legs and powerful flanks. The soldier hops out, leaps, dances about on his one long, one short leg, somersaults, flails his muscular arms. He is imitating Cordes. He is I, a cripple. I now see him full face for the first time. His face is young, strong, with the flattened nose of an Indian, his eyes dark, alive, quick. The cast of his mouth is happy, not sullen or cruel as I had expected. It is rarely if ever that happy people are also cruel. Cruelty and its sibling, excessive passivity, spring from the crotch of the identical disease—depression. He stops to piss, making a high arch, then speaks to his spout aloud, laughingly.

"Old bird, you have been neglected. Soon, soon, you will not look so dejected. I will find you a warm nest," giving it a playful slap, "and you will fly straight and proud." Tweaks it, laughs loud, happily. Happy slave.

Not yet wholly dry, he begins to dress, speaking aloud to himself, in the way of a man who is lonely. "That has been good, but it's time we move on, old horse."

Yes, he has replayed my own little game. We are, after all, kin, still I cannot shoot him in the back.

"¡Hola!" I call out.

With one motion he yanks his carbine from the scabbard and turns toward the bush, his bright eyes round in his dark, vital face as I step calmly into the open and cut his head in two with a burst. As he falls he does not even twitch. The mare had reared at the explosion and then whinnied loud, now she turns to stare at her fallen master with childish eyes, and continues her unhurried nibbling at the grass.

I approach her calmly, speaking softly to her, horses have been my playmates since birth, and she raises her long, soft face to stare at me, to await her new master. As I approach her, I trip over the soldier's fallen rifle, and the mare, affrighted by my sudden lurch, skitters and gallops off in the direction whence the soldier had come.

I curse vociferously, gaze at the dead soldier. I hate to kill men for no purpose.

38

V ————————————————

Only with purpose.

Still, purpose or not, I suffer no remorse, though I should if I did not bury him, but that is only because of a fastidiousness with which I suffer. I could not bear to think of his corpse exposed, blackening, decaying, food for vultures. To bury him is to give the deed symmetry. I drag him by his gimped leg to a depression in the ground, then gather stones to make a cairn for him. Some mark their way with poisoned darts, with arrows, I with cairns of stone. Before I cover his head I close his eyes by weighting their lids with flat pebbles. When one enters that long, black corridor one should be sightless so as not to see the evil at each winding. Not seeing is not to be seen.

I resume my trek into the puna. The bay mare will soon forget, stop to graze, and I will come upon her. If not, she will stop at the first horse she sights, seek out her own. A shepherd will strip her of her tack, conceal bridle, saddle, saddlebags, scabbard, and take her for his own. It will be assumed the soldier had deserted—an everyday occurrence. Now that he is buried I have forgotten him. That is my way—to bury what is unpleasant. A virtue for a man in my trade. Of course, his round, fearful eyes had stared into mine for an unforgettable moment, but I am peopled with many eyes, though they visit with me only in those rare times when I dream. There are the hating eyes lost in the black face of a Congolese—but I desire not to speak of it. There are the eyes of a former comrade in the peninsular fighting, soft, brown, uncomprehending.

"Why?" his eyes cried.

Why, indeed. I did not myself squeeze the trigger. There are squads for this. Their reward? Medals struck for HEROES OF THE PEOPLE.

Eyes, eyes, I am pocked with eyes. Buteo's eyes and the monomaniacal single eye of Schleimann whom I killed as a favor to U. Intense blue, blood-flecked, pupil dilated, fiercely courageous, but totally mad. Had been U's slave for thirty years because he believed him to be the only man capable of leading them to power in Germany. Had undertaken the most hideous tasks, had been one of the few men courageous enough to join the S.S. as U's agent. Had survived every filth, only to become weak ten years after the seizure of power. "I thought the filth would purify us, make us immune, only to discover we are in the same garbage heap. Ja! we have made one great advance. We have learned to rid the garbage of flies. BUT THE STINK IS THE SAME!" Stupid fool. Soon the flies would return bigger and stronger than ever. U pleaded personal embarrassment. "I would prefer *ein Ausländer* to do it—there is unrest among my own." An outsider, I did him this favor, about which I have learned to feel remorse. Not over Schleimann's death, but because U marked it in his little book for future use. When Marguerite was selected to seduce me into submission to their discipline, she warned me they would not be loathe to accuse me of murder if I refused. I laughed. "And drive me to Peking?" At which she blanched with fear.

There is nothing like a little competition.

I met her shortly after Dzugashvili and Broz quarreled and Markos disappeared, the Greek revolution as much a victim as he. What the cowardly D could not control he sought to destroy. Broz, inflamed by his own rage at being dominated, administered him a defeat the repercussions of which will continue for half a century.

I fled to France who generously offers her naked breasts like clusters of rich fruit equally to would-be conquerors, charlatans and revolutionaries. Marguerite there on a holiday, assigned to woo me. In Greece I had revealed a fine revolutionary sensitivity and had developed the feasibility of utilizing adolescent boys and girls in roving bands—wild, ruthless, daring, yet, like young dogs, responsive to a strong master hand. Later, on the peninsula, after victory, we used similar bands to control the adult population. Cruel, perhaps, but extremely effective. When adolescents contributed so fiercely to the defeat of France in Algiers, the name of Ramón Cordes was accorded sanctification at a black mass held on the streets of the *rive gauche*.

But at that time, after the Greek disaster, I fled to Paris. There, a young barbarian among the paladins of the international intellectual left, I was ensconced in a splendor equal to, perhaps surpassing, that I had left at home—their books sold in the millions—and felt as uneasy as would the young Christ in a Claudian palace on the banks of the river Tiber. A gun availed me naught. I coughed and I bled as I had begun to cough and to bleed in the house of my family shortly before I absconded to join the revolution in Greece. Uneasy, and then terrified. For it was from them I learned that for a revolutionary every defeat is victory and every victory defeat. The struggle is eternal. One night, my lean weight impressed on a bed softer than any I had ever known, my taste buds still overflowing with aromatic spices from the most delectable foods I had ever eaten, my mind distraught, overwrought, frightened, my blood tingling, I came to the realization that I had in truth chosen the path singularly right for me. I was the revolution—for me there could be no victories and no defeats, only struggle.

Marguerite. I avoid her.

I thought her lovely then: slender, dark, with sensual lips and brooding eyes, her short black hair wild, tousled in the fashion of the time, her handcrafted Mexican leather bag slung over one shoulder as a balance to the accentuated slope of the other. Her walk was a strange mix of stroll, amble, lope and slink. As a young English boy once unabashedly cried out in an afternoon crowd on Boul' Mich, "Look, Mother, that woman looks like a walking leaning tower of Pisa." Half smiling, I glanced at Marguerite out of the corner of an amused eye and saw her face remain impassive, though she did bite her lower lip and make an effort, almost successful, to walk as most humans do. As we turned a corner, she took my face between her gentle hands and kissed me hard on the lips.

An open invitation to a blank wall. Though apparently free, sensual, willing and wanting, she did not permit me to sleep with her for many weeks. "Not yet,

Ramón. I am not a public cup." Lenin's words, of course. But I soon learned it was not Leninist virtue as much as fear of self-revelation.

And though we did not make love or sex, we talked.

"You're envious of them," she said. We had spent the evening at a party given in my honor—a hero of the Greek revolution—on rue Jacob with numerous writers and philosophes, ideologues of revolt and violence. They spoke of revolution with passionate fervor, yet I detected a fatuous arrogance among them. It made me ill. They were the brain of the revolution; the masses, the defeated, the slaves were the limbs, the appendages to be commanded by the brain. I brought it to their attention. One man, many years my senior, dark, gleaming face, sloping shoulders, eyes fat with conceit, stomach puffed with self-love, stared at me incredulously. "But, Ramón," he almost patted my head, "that is a fact of our existence we must accept. The lumpen are atomized, the masses stupefied by exploitation. Only we, educated by, yet excluded from, our society, have the ability to see. The wish to see. The energy. The will. Why should we abdicate?" Yes, indeed. It was because I agreed with him that I became enraged. I stood up to face him. Were we forever doomed by the past? Conquerors and conquered; manipulators and manipulated? I stared at the man with hatred. Though lean-faced, he had a huge paunch—a thin man growing from a fat. I remembered having read in a Freudian essay that within every fat man crouches a thin paranoiac. I couldn't help but smile through the rage. I stared into his eyes puffed with arrogance, his intelligence already fat with power before he even got to wield it, and then said what has already earned me canonization among

43

my followers and suspicion from the orthodox like Rojos, "Comrade, concealed within every burning revolutionary stands a flaming fascist." Everyone at the party was struck dumb. Then S, who though sitting across the room had heard everything, blinked his eyes behind his thick glasses, and said quietly, "A brilliant insight, Ramón. Brilliant! We must discuss it further some day." "Yes," I said with a self-conscious laugh, "it is one of our own inner contradictions." And everyone applauded. I smiled acknowledgment. Became gay. Had won points in a parlor game. Now Marguerite and I, arm in arm, were ambling, loping, slinking to her hotel, the magnificent Meurice. Marguerite is herself an intelligent revolutionary: she demands the best for herself.

"Of course, I envy them."

"They are intellectually superior, their erudition vast, Ramón."

"Yes, it is obvious—they assert it so loudly."

She smiled with secret knowledge, which she then shared. "You're afraid of being dominated by them."

"By them, or anyone else. Absolutely."

"You are also jealous of their power."

"Yes; you see me clearly."

"Yet I could see you have greater ambition and pride than they."

I laughed. She had good eyes. "Obviously. You saw how many of them, brilliant, erudite, nearly everyone of whom had fought in the Resistance, slavered at my feet simply because I had fought under the red banner in Greece. And I think it's the color red which excites them so, not what I fought for."

"You enjoyed your tyranny over them. You also are a burning revolutionary concealed in whom . . ."

44

"Exactly."

She forced me to stop and to turn to look at her. Her face was agitated, serious, dark; she was not playing games. "What do you mean exactly?"

I started to take her into my arms, and for a moment, weak, she clung, then evaded me. "Answer me, please."

"Envy, jealousy, fear of domination coupled with a strong wish to dominate, to tyrannize, ambition and great pride—it is precisely for these reasons that I have become a revolutionary."

She wet her lips nervously, began to breathe more quickly, her hands trembled, her bright eyes searched mine. "It is not for justice?"

I choked off the laugh in my throat and turned to continue ahead. Her thin fingers clutched at my elbow. "Ramón!"

"Justice is for children, Marguerite."

She withdrew her hand swiftly as if burned. "You seek power!"

I laughed. "I hate and am afraid of power."

Now she smiled, for she had found what she sought. "Exactly," she said, mimicking accurately my tone of voice.

I remained silent. We strolled along the river for an hour, aimlessly, silently, each with his own thoughts, no doubt. Then spent a strange night in her room. She asked me to stay, to sleep in the same bed with her, to hold her in my arms—she was thinner than I expected, though well-formed, long, elegant, as seen and felt through a diaphanous gown—but nothing more. I told her it was obscene, we weren't children, were both free, but she pleaded with me to forgive her, to merely embrace her, and I finally yielded to her wishes, piqued in a way by the sensuality of abstinence. We embraced, kissed, innocently, like two children.

I woke before dawn. The room was shrouded in a gray darkness. The curtains billowed at an open window. Outside, it rained, a light drizzle, the air smelled fresh, clean. Only her face protruded from the eiderdown quilt, her black hair tousled wildly about her head. Her face was pointed, thin, bony, pale, like that of a wild dog, and in repose and all innocence her lips curled cruelly—a cruelty born from a secret, terrible hunger. My impulse was to take her, to give myself to her, fiercely, without restraint. Totally. To devour and be devoured. But she moved, turned to her side, and the cast of her face changed to one of utter tenderness. And the impulse was gone as quickly as it had come.

I rose, bathed, dressed and left.

Later in the day I received a note from her. She had gone to one of the beaches in the south, would I join her there in a week's time? In a fury at the obviousness of her game I tore the note to confetti for our silly parade.

She waited for me as I stepped from the train, the arrivals and departures mingling virginal whiteness with professional tans, the sea off to the side unseen, signaling its presence with surging breath. Her dark legs rose slenderly from leather sandals to scant skirt which hugged her narrow waist and long torso hidden by a loose sleeveless blouse under which I could see her small breasts move unbound. Her long throat rose from sloping shoulders to pointed face in one graceful sweep, scribing her thin lips and aquiline nose to her large, darkling eyes.

We kissed like lovers, and I could feel her lips trembling. She quivered like a fern, the perfume subtle, I myself recalcitrant.

"You're angry, Ramón."

"It appears we're embarked on a childish game."

"I am not playing a game."

"What is this virginal coyness if not a game?"

"I'm neither a virgin, nor coy, and I'm not playing a game. I have a right to make sex or love when I feel I will enjoy it."

"I agree with you, but that's not your reason. They've sent you after me—want to chain me like a dog to their kennel. I won't be chained."

She pulled away. "It's not important. Let's go to the car." Said with an indifferent shrug, and so off-handedly that I quite believed her. I had not yet learned that when she said something was not important that was precisely when it was.

Marguerite drove me in her little red Lancia through the white oleander, the cypress, the red hibiscus, the cascading willows, to a minuscule pink villa reclining in a glade above an inlet of the sea. On these winding roads, in this refuge of the rich, the red Lancia was just another little sports car among the many. But in the capital of Buteo's land, in the mountains, the villages of the puna, it was a sleek, red arrow pointing in one direction. Ramón Cordes.

Behind the ancient stone walls concealed by mimosa, trumpet vines and golden day lilies, in the refreshing coolness of shade overhead and tile underfoot, we explored one another. Our tenderness belied our feral intent and our fear betrayed our obvious sophistication. Each day we strove for discovery, first with gentleness, softness, patience, her eyes large, huge in their bright

47

blackness, her thin lips swollen, her slender body an un-
sprung coil. She wished to yield, and I to conquer. Yet I
loathed conquest and she to be supine. Then, failing,
still alien to each other, we began to rip and tear, to
storm, only to be trapped in a wallow, a mire, an aching
nothingness.

"It is not only one against the other," I whispered, "it
is also each against himself."

Exhausted, frowning, pale, she remained silent.
Then, afraid to acknowledge defeat, she attempted a
smile. Forlorn. "Why? What's wrong?" False innocence.

"Stop pretending, Marguerite."

"It's not important," she snapped. "For God's sake,
it's not important." Her lips became thin, cruel, and her
pointed, bony face had again assumed that look of a
wild dog, and my first impulse was to strike her.

Instead I sighed. "You're right," I said. "Let's forget
it."

Only to begin afresh the following day. A swim in the
cove, a brisk shower, Schubert on the record player, an
ample breakfast served by a felt-slippered maid, obse-
quious, round-backed, an unhappy reminder of home.
Sprawled under the sun, intermittently reading, talking,
touching, energy restored, a sudden kiss, an intimate caress, and we were again catapulted into battle. Insane
battle, senseless. We should have yielded, surrendered.
Perhaps we were too proud. Perhaps we possessed a su-
perfluity of courage, that is to say, we were battle foolish, oblivious of the danger, victory no longer the aim,
sought out the battle for its own sake, to sow cruelty and
harvest wounds.

We shared hatred. Soon I could not endure the touch

48

of her, her scent, the thinness of her body, the wild dog look of her face. I began to make excuses to go to the village, and she, it must be said, was pleased to have me go. One afternoon I met a mature woman at the beach and found surcease in her arms, her breasts, her wifely body, calmly, gently, sweetly. No victory, equal surrender. We parted reluctantly, each having given so generously that to separate truly meant to leave part of ourselves with the other.

"When?" I asked before parting.

She touched my cheek tenderly with her fingers. "No."

"Why not?"

"I love another."

"Then why this?"

"It has been a long time and he is bored, I suppose. He ignores me."

"Why don't you leave him?"

She pursed her generous mouth a moment, stared at me with questioning eyes. "Is it really that simple?" Then left. I followed her full, vigorous, wifely figure with saddened eyes.

When I returned to the villa, Marguerite, darkly elegant in white slacks and blue jersey shirt open to her navel, slinking, leaning, greeted me hoarse-voiced. "Where were you? Why were you gone so long?"

I told her, awaited the onslaught, the rage, the tears. Instead she flushed with excitement, smiled warmly, took my hand and kissed it softly.

For a few days we basked in the warm, loving glow of generosity. But then I suppose the competitive edge wore off, I was only hers, and since she could not abide that, we were soon crouched on our battlefield—no,

49

worse, in an insane asylum, the straitjackets just loose enough to give us room to tear ourselves to shreds on the wet leather thongs.

"Goodbye," I said coldly, bag in hand, as she stared up at me from the tile terrace to which I had thrown her in a quiet rage a good fifteen minutes before. An actress, she had a fine talent for melodrama. She lay languidly, gracefully, her face darkly flushed, lips moist, nose flaring, acting out her chosen role. A Hollywood forgery. Double fake. She had sweetly suggested I find the woman and invite her to the villa.

Ever hopeful to bring me down and so perhaps lessen the stink of her own slime, she said accusingly, "You *are* inhibited, aren't you?"

"It's not important," I said with an icy smile, yet relenting enough to reach out my hand to her.

As she swung to her feet she threw herself into my arms, weeping, her lips wet on my shoulder, quivering like a frightened bird. If it had been possible I would have cupped her in my hands, sheltered her, soothed her. I felt pity for her, compassion, but could say nothing, merely permitted her to rest against me, her lips on my throat. Her trembling body in my arms felt as slight as a child's, but her hands on my back were fisted, the knuckles sharp, not from malice—no, she was beyond that now—from fear, that commonest of maladies, that plague, that affliction for which there is no vaccine, no antibiotic, no patent medicine, only an occasional word, an understanding smile, a solicitous caress. But I could find none to give. Merely stood like a post, on which she wept, whipped by the tears.

Until she stepped back, blinking her eyes clear, a crooked smile on her lacerated face. "Thanks," she said.

"For what?"

"You're kinder than you think."

"You are being sentimental, Marguerite. I give nothing."

"Yes, you do! You do!" An incantation to drive the evil spirit away. Ah, yes, there it is—witchcraft, the best cure for our little malady.

Even here on this grassy plateau. I've just coughed, just spat, and there it is, the blood glistening in the sun, a tiny drop floating in my sputum, life's substance, how incarnadine, a pelucid drop, red world bobbing in polluted liquid space. I am totally alone. Belong to no one; no one belongs to me. Unique on this temperate plateau between the tropical nether world of the valley and the arctic cathedral world of the mountain peaks, I cough and I spit blood. And rucksack on back, gun in hand, walk true west, death at my heels like a faithful dog. "Go," I command him. "GO!" And he heeds me. I smile. My nose has picked up a friendly scent, my feet have sunk into fresh alpaca manure. Ah, there it is—all about me. Fresh, still moist. A shepherd and his flock are close at hand.

I laugh, I run, following those little heaps of sweet dung.

There! A flock heavy with winter wool, the shearing and the mating are soon to begin. It is spring. Glorious spring.

And I forget the soldiers, the pursuit, the hour won, the loneliness, the fear. I shall sit under yon beautiful quebracho and share an hour as we eat sweet potatoes and oranges, I and the shepherd who now rises to greet me, his eyes fearful as he sees my gun.

VI

The gun. That filth.

I fling it aside with a flourish so he sees I mean no harm. I flip off my fatigue cap and it sails through a high arc to come to rest near the gun. Now the shepherd knows I have come as a friendly guest to sit with him under his tree. He makes me welcome with arms spread wide, palms up, and a dignified nod of swarthy head. He wears black full trousers tied about his ankles and waist with a string. The waist is very narrow. His camisa is white, also full, the sleeves full, ballooned, tight at the wrists. His hair is long and black, and the face hairless. A boy, I think.

As I approach, we read one another's eyes, searching for possible harm, for strength, for weakness. Simultaneously we smile, each satisfied that there will be peace between us.

We are now under the tree, face to face, and the shepherd is no boy but a girl. With high cheekbones, hawked slender nose, broad forehead, a wide mouth with rich, heavy lips, sombre, tranquil, the lips of a human being accustomed to solitude, whose life is solitude, who lives without chatter among her sheeplike flock surging about us, bawling, nibbling at the ichu grass, defecating, a dumb, undulating mass. She is sturdy, her feet broad in her sandals, but her waist narrow and her breasts vibrant under the white camisa.

She speaks to me in her dialect but comprehends immediately that I do not understand. Her voice is low, melodious, pleasant.

"I speak the tongue of the capital," I tell her.

"Yes, I understand, I have been taught by the priest in the village. But I speak my tongue first. You are a foreigner," she says, and I think it is like the mark of Cain on my forehead, so easily discerned. "It makes you unhappy?" She is perceptive, quick-witted, or my face is a video screen.

"It is not important," and I bite my tongue. Her eyes have not left mine for one moment. She continues to read, comprehends that I dissemble, but is kind.

"Forgive me, perhaps I am too forthright."

"No, no. Forgive me for not being as honest as you. Lies come too easily. Yes, it makes me unhappy to be seen immediately as a foreigner." And I can feel a flush rising to my face. "You have, incidentally," I add, "been taught, and learned, well."

"You have a beautiful beard," she says, smiling. Before I can respond, she asks, "Are you hungry?"

"I have food in my rucksack, but I am weary of it."

We sit under the quebracho and we eat alligator pears, caju, and drink wine from her gourd. It is very sour, almost as strong as whiskey, invigorating. My flask is emptied of its tequila and I tell her I would buy some wine from her and she says no, they have much, and fills it for me. I am silent as we eat, as is she. It is an

53

unembarrassed silence, it is a tranquillity under the shade of the tree, a cool freshness guarded from the high sun, the ichu grass rustling softly, the alpaca lolling, the shepherdess's body strong, uncoiled yet tensile, gracefully controlled, and she smells of caju, of strong wine, as we sit separated by inches, and I ache to touch her. No, not carnally, but with a strange, tender affection, an innocence almost. More, more. I cannot define it. It is new to me. It frightens me. I am resting easily alongside her yet I can feel myself trembling where it cannot be seen, deep inside myself. She moves an arm, lowers a leg, gracefully, calmly, she is without fear, she believes she has read me accurately, that my malice is subdued.

Witchcraft again? There must be a scientific answer. There absolutely must be. We cannot read the unseen. I lose patience with myself. Accept it. No. You are being gulled by the peasant mystique, Cordes. She lives close to the land, to the earth, and it tells her its secrets. Demeter perhaps whispers in her ear. We are returned to Greek mythology. I berate myself. Concede. She knows what I do not, what I cannot define.

As I am about to ask her, she says, "What is it?"

I feel myself blanch. I stare at her. Her heavy lips are firmed into a straight line, her nostrils flare, her eyes are quizzical, puzzled, the dark smoothness of her forehead marred now by questions. "I was just about to ask you what it is with me, for there is something I can't define."

"I listen often to the radio from the capital. A teacher there, a professor from the university, gives lessons and I learn, study. He reads books to us. Are you superstitious?"

I laugh. A fine question to ask of Ramón Cordes. "Merely overcome by your grace, your generosity."

Frowning, uncomprehending, she again asks, "Are you?"

"No, I'm not superstitious."

She nods, then remembers what I have said. "Generous? Because I have shared my fruit, my wine?"

"You have shared more than food."

For the first time she lowers her eyes, frowns, is disturbed. Her eyes shielded, she says, "You are very handsome."

"If I were ugly, would you have greeted me otherwise?"

She hesitates, turns her broad, bony face toward me, and I can see she is searching for the truth. She sighs deeply, her breasts quivering under the white camisa. "I would share my food with anyone," she says quietly, "but still, I don't think I would have greeted you so fully, so openly if you were not handsome. Perhaps that is wrong, but it is . . . aren't you pleased because I am . . ."

"Yes, because you are a lovely girl. That's true, yes. No, that is not wholly true. It is your generosity that moves me, that you are without fear, without evil. You are open, like the sky above the puna." I wish to go on but I see she is disturbed, her breathing comes with difficulty, and her swart cheeks are made even darker by the rush of blood. I desire to take her strong, broad hand in mine but abruptly she leaps to her feet, grabs up her crook and runs to her flock which is opening up at one arc of its circumference. She runs swiftly, her heels flashing among the tall grass. Utilizing her crook with brisk competence, speaking softly to them, she soon has her flock in a tight, closed ring. I observe admiringly, smoking my Havana.

She ambles toward me slowly, the crook on her

shoulder like a gun, and suddenly I remember the gimped soldier and his round, scared eyes and I close mine, struck with fear. Pursued, I tarry, infatuated with this robust, graceful girl. Her footsteps are close and I lift my tired, heavy head.

Her full, thick lips are solemnly drawn, the hollows under the high cheekbones flushed, her eyes worried. I have disturbed the peaceful calm of her existence.

"I must go," I say, not rising.

"You seem very tired," she says softly, and I can discern indecision in her voice. She wishes me to leave but also to stay.

I shake my head, giving her my hands to help me to rise. Hers are cool, strong, vibrant. As I stand close to her, her scent of fruit and wine, her vitality communicates itself to me, debouches the inertia, her generosity overwhelming me with life. We stand thus, our hands still clasped, otherwise not touching, feeling this fresh, open affection between us. (I am embarrassed. Cordes is afraid to say love.) "You have been kind," I whisper, "and I must leave. Be kind enough to let me go. I am after all only a stranger."

Simply, she places her head gently on my chest, and I hold her quietly to me, so she can feel my pulsating heart.

Abruptly, harshly almost, she withdraws. Stares questioningly, fearlessly, at me. Has she again read what I have not said but what lies concealed within my heart and head? "You are running!"

I have not lied to her, and will not. "Yes. Soldiers are searching for me."

"You are a brigand?"

"Yes, I suppose it can be said I am. I must go now," I

say briskly. "You have been kind, many thanks." Her eyes are large upon me as I bend to take up my rucksack, my cap, and gun.

"I will conceal you." Just like that.

I drop my things and take her head between my hands and stare into her candid eyes. She is a woman—free, and complete. But I must remember who I am, the way that I must go. "If they find me here, they will imprison your father, burn down his house, steal his flocks. Perhaps harm you." And my eyes flit over her body.

She stands, thinking, biting a fingernail. She is only a child. I am being romantic, blind.

"I remember now," she says. "The radio. You are Ramón Cordes. You must hide."

I smile at her with kindness. After two futile months in this country, my band demolished, Buteo dead, I have at last won a convert to my cause. It is ridiculous, this child . . .

My flask refilled with strong wine, my rucksack with caju, oranges, avocado, I quietly bid her goodbye. "I will reach the mountains by nightfall, and tomorrow the border. Then I will be safe. Be well, lovely one."

There she stands at the edge of her flock, crook in hand, her face immobile, stolid.

And I have squandered the hour.

VII

The sun, sharply defined like a full moon seen after night has vanished, makes its slow descent behind the mountains. A strange light is shed upon the snowy peaks, upon the mass of rock, upon the grassy plains of the puna. No longer God's hands futilely grasping for the unknown heaven, but heaps, masses, whole continents of humanity escaping the earth. They clamber, scramble, scratch, fight, slip, stumble, fall. Rise to resume their way. Rarely do they look back, yet when they do it is with nostalgia.

The puna is cool now, the green grass dark with shadow. An occasional cedar sends forth its scent as if to invite one for a night of sweet rest under its heavy boughs or a huge black walnut rich with its meaty fruit, Nut, mythological consort of the Earth.

Their nostalgia is heavy, but they do not turn back. The puna bores them, its immense plains too flat in contradistinction to the lush tropical valley below and the aspiring peaks above—the fruit, the peccary, the brook, the Indian shepherdess too easily accessible. Be my husband. I will be your wife. Nurture me in your arms and I will veil you in mine. The first commune.

They do not turn back. Neither do I. Paradise is for the dumb beast. We are too high and mighty for that. We aspire to the heavens. And in a hundred thousand years we have not advanced an inch. For wherever we are, there is hell.

It is suddenly dark. I am at the edge of the puna and at the first trail leading up into the mountain range. I smile with satisfaction at anticipated escape. I hear the neighing of a horse. Drop swiftly, silently to the ground. Wait, breath quickened. Listen, my skin taut. Again a horse neighs; paws at the ground; swishes its tail at the insects. I can see nothing. I advance quietly on elbows and knees, the gun cradled in my arms. A hiss close to my ear. Startled, I turn. I am side to side with a snake as long as my arm. Harmless, he slithers into the brush. I advance. Discern white markings on fetlocks and recognize the spindly legs of the bay mare. Controlling my elation, I rise cautiously at her side, clasp the loose reins, whisper softly into her ear. "You are a beauty, I will treat you well." She whinnies her affection, for she is a vain child, though well-mannered and strong. She is mine! I stake her to a tree. And dance. It will cut my time to the border in half. "You're a beauty, a beauty," I cry, throwing my arms about her neck, kissing her soft muzzle. She whinnies and neighs, skittering about on her spindly ankles, happy to have found a companion, for horses detest loneliness, how strange.

I make camp under a colo, among bunch grass, a coarse ichu. As I proceed up the mountain the vegetation will become scantier until I reach the snowline by which time there will be none. But now I have a horse.

My nylon sleeping bag, an expensive gift from a North American admirer when I lived on the peninsula, unrolled, I sit down, remove my shoes, massage my feet, refresh my face and hands with water from my canteen. Contented, I eat cheese, the caju, the avocado given to me by the Indian girl, and drink her strong wine. Tonight I will sleep well, as now I eat well, and I will dream of my shepherdess, my head couched between her young breasts, my pistolet scabbarded in her sheath. Before I turn in, I again speak to my horse, embrace her, whisper words of love, ascertain that the stake is secure.

Weary, it has been a long day, I slip into the blanket roll, zip myself and gun in, turn to sleep. I should sleep soundly for I know that tomorrow I will be at the border, and then into safety. I sigh, close my eyes, but sleep evades me. False optimism. Blindness. There will be no dreams, only reality. There it is, all about me, it clings, suffocates me, it is the stench of decay. The defeat. I should say *my* defeat but find it too difficult. I refuse to face it, to stare it in the eye. As soon as I begin to think about it, an eel, it slips away. Raises its bullet-like head as if to taunt me. I clench my fists, close my eyes, and it wraps itself about my leg. I ignore it, it will go away, disappear into the watery murkiness, lose itself in the seaweed. It unwinds from my leg, slithers upward, nudges me in the ribs. I grab for it to choke it to death, it is not there. It has gone to slumber under the sunken hull of a sloop. Gone, it does not exist. I forget about it. Enjoy a moment of peace. Screech with a semi-moronic giggle, for it has goosed me in the ass.

FACE IT! Defeat the defeat. For once in your bloody life face up to it.

Other things, other times. It is night, the house is asleep, even the servants. Father has gone to the city for the night. I cannot sleep. I sit at the window to stare into the darkness. I am a thin, nervous little boy. Ten years old. The only sound is that of the horses as they stamp about in their nightly search for a weak section of the fence through which to break out. The paint gelding is exceedingly cunning. He has learned to nudge the gate latch loose with his muzzle, but the stableman has this very afternoon nailed it to. Yet I am certain, and perversely hope, that the sly gelding will find a way. When one breaks loose, they all follow, galloping across the meadows until they encounter another herd at pasture. There they hold council for a few moments amid neighs and whinnies and pawing of earth, then altogether gallop off to the next ranch, again hold parley, and off all through the night until the morning when they are a herd of hundreds, whinnying, pawing, biting, kicking, bucking in the meadow grass, free for a few hours until the ranchers, a smaller herd, peccant, come upon them to bribe with sweet feed, and it consumes hours for each to pick out his own and lead them back to their barns and paddocks. For a few days they are quiescent, herbivorous beasts ignorant of their great strength. I have pity for them and also contempt. Nothing will hold me, I say. This night as I sit at the window, father gone, the house quiet, dark, I hear a door open, it is past midnight, then close; footsteps in the corridor, down the carpeted stairs, across the hall, out the door. My eyes are intense, see in the darkness: it is my mother in her riding habit. I am tempted to call out, "Where are you going, Mother?" but stay my tongue. She enters the barn and I can hear her booted feet on the wooden floor, the sound of impatient hooves. Shortly she reappears leading what I discern to be the buckskin stallion, sire

61

of the cunning paint. He is impatient, frisks about. She embraces his long neck, and she is whispering to him, I know, as she strokes his underbelly until he is quiet, stands arrogantly, head high. Clutching his mane she leaps gracefully to mount him, walks him slowly to the field, then, under a luminous midnight sky they gallop off, claimed by the vast plains, the night.

For an incomprehensible reason I become frightened, my breath short, quick, as if my mother has asserted her freedom, forced a final separation from my father, me, my older brothers and sisters—we shall never see her again. I wish to cry out to her, "Mother, where are you going? Come back!" but a terrifying inertia imprisons me, my lungs are bursting and I am trembling, dizzy with fear, my mouth and lips dry, tongue large and clumsy. Somehow I force myself to the door, grasping at consciousness with clenched teeth.

The cool night air revives me. The ache of fear is acute, no longer vague. I stub a naked toe, the paint gelding rattles the gate. With a sob I begin to run across the meadow in the direction my mother has taken. The stubble rips at my bare feet. They bleed but I do not feel them. I am conscious of another pain, a murderous fear, the night air cold and moist on my thin body under my pajamas, and a solitude, a vast interminable solitude opens before me and it is like a huge vacuum pressing upon me, closing out all air, bursting my lungs, and blood gushes through my nose, my mouth, and I scream after her to return, not to leave me, us, that I will be good, will be good, until I stumble, fall to the ground exhausted. Troubled sleep. Then peace.

I am in the garden. The sun is hot, languid. Myriad flowers are in bloom, the colors extravagant, rich. No sooner is a petal in decay than the gardener snips it. No rot must disturb the beauty before our eyes. We are reclining on the grass, my mother and I. My eyes are closed so that all is shut out but her breathing—dulcet, soft. She is writing on a note pad. I drowse. Shortly I am wakened by the touch of something on my knee. It is my mother's pad, she has fallen asleep, her breast softly rising and falling, her scent sweet, that of the grass fresh, cool. I take the booklet in my hand. At the head of the first leaf are the words "A Fable." I smile. She has, I think, written a fable for me. I begin to read it.

In an arid, mountainous country, on a promontory ledge no wider than a man's shoulders, a thin, swart peasant has found a few meters of soil. He lives below in a mud hut with his comely wife and small children. As he tills the soil, she weaves baskets. Every day he fills the baskets with red clay from the valley and large leather gourds with water from a narrow, shallow stream that winds through a scrub oak wood. Baskets and gourds balanced on either side of his donkey's ridged, bony back, he leads it up the footpath to his ledge. A straw hat protects him from a fierce white sun as with a hoe he mixes the soil with clay, and then on hands and knees constructs miniature irrigation ditches into which he empties the gourds of their water. For fertilizer he uses human ordure. He seeds his ledge with chickpeas, beans, onions. Thus he creates life from stone. Without question he understands it is his purpose to live and give life.

At noon he sits in the scant shade of a stunted gnarled oak and slowly eats a huge slab of bread with a salted onion, washed down with sour red wine. Then he curls up beneath the tree and sleeps until four o'clock when the torpid sun begins its descent. Refreshed, he resumes his labor on another ledge that he has begun to nurture.

His seed takes root, his children grow, in season his wife fills the baskets with his harvest, loads the donkey and takes their produce to the provincial market, where she converses with her friends and sells her goods.

One day, another ledge tilled and nurtured, having eaten his bread and onion, drunk from his wine gourd, as he is about to curl up beneath a tree, he hears his wife cry out down below. With a leap he snatches up his hoe and runs frantically down the path. As he enters his hut the peasant sees a stranger atop his disheveled wife. Enraged, he beats the stranger with his hoe, and kills him. His wife flees into the mountain to hide in shame.

The peasant flings the dead man across his donkey's back and leads the animal with its burden through the valley to the local police to whom he explains what has occurred. Later his wife corroborates his simple story and the peasant is released.

His comely wife and he resume their daily existence without interruption or change. When, many months later, his wife gives birth to another child, the peasant does not question her. If he has any doubts he in no way indicates it. The child is alive, innocent, and must be nurtured.

As I conclude reading the tale, my mother still asleep beside me, I see for the first time my father standing tall above us. His gleaming boots are blinding from the torpid sun.

Encased in the warm sleeping bag, I stare into the night, the trees towering above me, casting grotesque dancing figures as they sway under a nocturnal breeze. I am exhausted, frightened, alone, the gun my sole companion. I am a grown man, one who knows defeat is real, death reality.

VIII

I am wakened from a heavy, torporlike sleep by the whinny of a horse. At first I believe it is the bay mare but in an anxious nerve-tearing moment I learn it is not. It comes from above me. Two horses. A loud whinny, then another. Now the bay mare answers. Soon they are in a loud snorting communication. The bay begins to buck and rear at her stake. I seize the decision swiftly. Leap to my feet, unstake the bay, slap her hard on the flank, off she gallops into the puna. The beat of the hooves above changes rapidly from walk to trot. They are close by. I throw my things into the sleeping bag, grab it up and glide into a glade of white pine where I take a position hidden by trees, tall grass and heavy bush. It is early dawn, gray, silhouettes sharp. I decide not to shoot when they appear for fear that farther along the trail are other riders. Out into the open of the plateau I see the bay mare has stopped to graze. My ears strain—the hoofbeats have ceased! Silence but for bird cries, flutter of wings. Intelligently, they have decided to reconnoiter. Must be soldiers. Alert, I wait. Not even the turning of a twig. Nothing. A lark sings. Silence. Seconds are an eternity. I am grimly alert, but fear has vanished. They are only men.

Above me, fifty feet perhaps, a horse neighs. I smile. Restrain a gasp, for ten feet to my side, knife clenched between teeth, gun cradled in arms, a soldier is crawling. I hold my breath, train my gun on his head, wait. In a few moments he is at the edge of the puna and spies the bay mare. Surprise slackens his jaws, and the knife falls to the earth. The soldier is soon on his feet, calling to his companion, "*Hola, hola*, the cripple has lost his horse!" From my seclusion, I grin at them.

As they stand together with their horses near the bay, I recognize them as two of the five horsemen of yesterday. They confer. As the shorter of the two speaks the other shakes his head negatively, points toward the area where I am hidden. The shorter now raises his gun and I am about to terminate his brief, harsh life when I realize he is going to shoot his gun into the heavens as signal only. The second soldier stops him. It would obviously be a signal not only to their cohorts somewhere in the mountains, but also to whomever they are seeking. Me. I can't help but smile. Strangely, though I am fearful, I enjoy this game. It is far superior to loneliness. Death so near, life surges buoyantly through my veins. I never cease wondering at how full of energy I become, at how playfully life pinches my pink little soul and tweaks my middle-aged genitalia at the very moment the grave opens before me.

The game must be played to the end.

I settle down into my lair. Instinctively I had chosen a perfect battle position. Survival is my forte. I was born to lead and to rule. To find me they will have to come directly upon me. If they do I am confident they will die before I do. The confidence yields me pleasure. One pleasure breeds another: if fortune turns perverse and they do kill me, they are murderers since they are, after all, the lickspittle of the ruling class; if I kill them, I am a hero since I am a revolutionary. History, a card sharp, stacks the cards: in either case they are murderers and I a hero.

It is as simple as that.

The two soldiers confer further. It is obvious to me the taller of the two is anxious for them to mount and depart. But the short soldier speaks more quickly, more profusely, and convinces him they have much time. I have an intuitive suspicion the tall soldier will learn to regret his comrade's persuasion.

I rest easily on my elbows, the gun trained on the two soldiers. The three horses tethered, they sit, legs crossed, break bread, drink wine, talk, ignorant of the rising sun behind them. It is hardly a dialogue, for the taller is a listener, his broad, stub face grim, and the shorter a compulsive talker, the words pouring from his scooplike face, little mouth, flat nose and foolish eyes sunk between a large protuberant forehead and square, jutting jaw. Though I hear him clearly, I do not understand him for he speaks now in an Indian dialect. The listener's grim face breaks into a silent laugh, the talker squirts spit from the side of his little mouth, shrugs and continues his endless chatter.

Soon I observe the listener is not listening, his eyes focus on nothing, stare into blank space, his mind a void. The talker, heedless, entranced perhaps by the epiglottal gurgling in his throat, scoops out words by the thousands. I already detest him. Still they are companionship of a sort, better than none.

68

Though we are, each in his own way, merely passing time, my ears and eyes remain alert, at constant attention. Obviously they are waiting for someone or something; perhaps a signal. They certainly do not appear anxious to leave my presence. Even unseen, my vaunted charisma works its mystique.

The sun is rising, beads of perspiration join to form a necklace under my cap, the birds chatter, call, whistle, take wing into a pale blue sky, a flash of red, of purple; sundry rodents—a field mouse, a vole, a mole—skitter by, stop, stare, scurry into a hole; a marsh hawk circles, dips a wing, vanishes. At the edge of the puna the listener listens, stares into space, the talker alternately spits and pours words, my detestation proliferating from single cell to lump to malignancy run wild. A mighty dominance, a dictatorship of words. Soon I will have to put an end to that word factory, burn it down, demolish it before its overproduction inundates the earth.

The sun, a shattered yellow eye, is halfway to its zenith. My hands become numb from their too tight clasp of the gun. I flex them until they tingle, return to life. Drink from my canteen, eat an orange. Unzip my fly, urinate slowly into the ground.

The two soldiers wait for their message. I wait with them. Their signal will also be mine. Ignorant though they are of my presence, they are joined to me by collective time and circumstance. History has given us benediction. We are brothers.

In the distance, to the northwest, a shot rings out. Answered by a burst. Another burst. My heart leaps. Only the type of gun I hold in my hand can fire a burst that quickly with that sound. A single shot—a carbine.

Two bursts. Friends. Comrades. My loyal friend has sent replacements. My heart expands with joy. The two soldiers have risen to their feet. Speak hurriedly. Run to the horses. I stand, the gun solid, certain in my hand.

"Soldiers!" I call in my survivor's voice, arrogant. I have no time for them. They turn frantically, stand open-mouthed. I shoot them down. The listener stares into space, into nothing; Scoopface's last gurgle, "Aieee!", dies in mid-air.

Silence at the edge of the puna.

I declare my identity to the distance. One shot, pause, three shots. I receive my answer. We will meet halfway.

I kiss my gun, hug myself, do a little jig.

Death must wait. I have won a battle.

IX

Astride the bay, who earlier saved my life, the horses of the two soldiers on a lead, I race across the edge of the puna north, the mountains to the west shielding us with their monumental quietude. To the east the sun still rises out of the valley, liquid. The enormous sky is purple, except where the sun dominates, there it is deliquescent red, blue, gold. The day, now that I am on the move, is crisp, the wind as I ride swiftly, bold. It will be an eventful day.

My comrades will be fresh with news from the capital, the peninsula, the world. We shall plan a daring campaign, throw caution to the crows. Let the vultures feed. We shall pillage and burn, destroy the old, take only the young; their life not yet begun, giving it no value, they risk it without thought. As do I. It is only the old who, investment long, coddle the years.

The gait of the bay is smooth, her mouth soft and sensitive to the bit. We fly. And I laugh. I think of the shepherdess, her fresh beauty, her firm breasts frolicking under the white camisa. She is a solid piece and I shall sink my roots in this country through her.

Marguerite and Rojos will eat their gall. Especially Rojos. He is slow, patient, impenetrable, implacable. One never knows what is concealed under that high dome. Those who know him say he decided on the day he was born to pattern his life after the fable of the hare and the tortoise. To the cautious, victory. So has it been. For thirty years hares have raced past him only to be clubbed to death. He has gone his way in the movement slowly, cautiously, never once having been heard to utter one word that could be said to be divisive, off-center. An orthodox, conservative man, he lives by one motto: when in doubt, wipe out.

Over the years hares have come, and hares have gone: defeated, defected, murdered by the police, by Rojos. Now in this land he is the movement. Pervasive, inexorable. Follows the line, despises the talkers like my loyal friend, fears the romantics like myself, Ramón Cordes, because he believes we can destroy in one month what has taken him thirty years to build: the myth that the party never loses—only men lose. Rojos believes he has great insight into romantic revolutionaries, especially Cordes. Bourgeois adventurers; bored with our existence, sated with things, artifacts, love, we seek excitement through the ultimate—a tilting with death. A simplification, perhaps, but not far from the truth—yet not far from the truth is much too far. Rojos lacks the imagination to comprehend, to encompass the x—the unknown factor, unique, mysterious, which makes me wish to fly, but not alone like a swooping hawk, but like a lark among an exaltation of larks. I wish to fly and to sing and to have man—and womankind—fly and sing with me. Yes, I plead guilty, Rojos. For this I have marked my trail with cairns of stone. Those two soldiers. Pocked, I am pocked with the eyes of the dead. And am fearful.

Still Rojos, the tortoise, the dinosaur, is cunning. He chose Marguerite for the task.

Between Cannes and the valley below we met often: in Algiers, the peninsula, Hanoi, even the Congo—Marguerite does not lack for courage—bearing messages and gifts. Not to me—to those in power or seeking power. In our world we are accepted as lovers. For me sex, love, is a moment of relaxation. Nothing more. All my energies are devoted to the cause—no more, no less than that of a warrior-monk to the Christ. I exult in the struggle. Sex, love, is a way station, a roadside inn, a stop for a night, a kiss, a clutch, an expiration, sleep. Good morning, breakfast, till next time. Off. With all her pretense at being a living, breathing vagina, that is all it is for Marguerite as well. She lives and breathes revolution—it is her very existence. She detests her family, her class, and loves her people. She will bring them justice if it means her life—or theirs. But, unlike me, she is afraid to fly. As is Rojos. He because there are no limits in flight, defeat is always imminent, a broken wing and disaster is complete. He has little faith, except in himself, though that is a contradiction. Feet on ground, two steps forward, one back. A tortoise, immortal, he has forever. She because she fears flight itself, afraid of the fall. Afraid of hell. Afraid of the earth—it may quake, erupt, open and swallow her. She bears the collective guilt of the millenia. Thus she holds on to the tortoise for very life—still, still, she yearns for the lark, reaches out for him—and sees hell.

She had come three days before with word that the

mine had reopened and that among the miners were comrades who wished to join us. Happy news. She brought provisions, ammunition, twenty additional guns—Russian subs, accurate, murderous. First she had come to a small village in the altoplana in her red Lancia, then had hiked fifteen miles to the Portal (though slight, she is resilient), where she was met by Armas whose turn it had been to be gateman. In a jeep he had returned with her during the night to the village, loaded the supplies, driven to the Delivery Room, ten miles west of the Portal, transferred to horses and donkeys and traveled through the night to our temporary camp in the valley.

When she entered my leanto under the trees, I was already up, having been wakened long before by the squawking macaws' electronic music. In her inimicable, melodramatic fashion she threw her tense self into my recalcitrant arms. I unpeeled her.

"Not now. First the news."

She stared at me with pain, sadly, and I was about to apologize for my rudeness—she looked woefully beautiful—when, a dying swan, a limpid ballerina, she fell back on my cot, and the words died on my tongue. I managed to suppress a smile. A hard, nasty, toughened revolutionary, professional, yet she had never been able to liberate herself as a woman. There she sprawled on my cot, panting. "You must be starved," she said, ridiculously wetting her lips with her tongue, a carmine snake. Her pointed, fawnlike face was thin, deeply tanned, and her eyes large, dark, brooding, their intensity heightened, not diminished, by lacelike wrinkles at their corners. Time was being generous with Marguerite.

"Not starved at all. On a campaign I have no need of women. My penis, like my energy, points in only one direction. Our enemy. Besides, here, as you know, we share equally." I smiled affectionately. She'd come so far, brought us riches.

"I'm willing," she laughed, settling herself comfortably on her back, her body lean in the riding jeans, yet soft, relaxed like a cat. I expected her to bend forward and begin licking herself.

"Fine. I'll go tell them. Even the two queers like a woman on occasion."

She sat upright. "All right, Ramón, I surrender."

"Must we always play your idiotic little game first? What's the news?"

"No news. Rojos said you're to clear out."

"You told me that the last time."

Now she smiled, but without humor, with a touch of malice. "Since the last time it has become even more apparent that your campaign is a disaster. You—"

"That's what they always say."

"You've gained nothing. Not one peasant has joined you, not even consented to feed you. It is injurious to our prestige—in the capital everyone is laughing."

"Parochial laughter. Little men, little vistas. Theo's come from Paris, brought greetings. The revolution is larger than just one country." It was the same old argument. I turned my back on her, impatient.

"Don't be rude!" Faced her again. "Thank you."

"Sorry."

"Yes, you're sorry." She was speaking for Rojos, and that gave her strength. "We're not interested in philosophical verbiage spilled like cognac on the little marble-topped tables of St.-Germain-des-Prés. Even though it's from a cobwebbed bottle of Napoléon. You're headed for disaster, Ramón. They're laughing at you."

"Me? Ramón Cordes is in China."

"They know you're here. It has your style."

"They laughed on the peninsula, too, before we buried them."

"True. And in the Congo."

"That was a lost battle before we—"

"You have a fatal attraction for lost causes."

"Naturally. That is why I fell in love with you."

She sat silently for a few moments under the sunlight that was pouring into the leanto, an early gold sun. I could see anger rising in her face. Her lips became a thin, red line, embattled under the sun, her eyes venomous. She sat straight, tensed. Yes, Rojos had chosen cunningly. With her, love and hatred shared a narrow single bed. I observed her as she was deciding what next to say. The decision made, she said it straight, frontally. "I'll ask you what no one else ever dares. Tell me, when you decided at the age of twenty to tear the earth apart, why didn't you begin in your own country as most men would?"

"Shut up, we're not discussing me."

"Why did you run from it, what is there that frightens you so?" Her pointed face was set harshly, vicious.

"How many guns did you bring?"

"You went to Greece where even if the revolution had won you could not. You were a foreigner!"

"You better rest. I'm going out to my men. We eat together."

She was on her feet, standing close to me, spitting words into my face. "Revolutions in their very guts are nationalistic, and you know it. The Greek revolution

76

failed, Markos failed, not you. You went elsewhere."

"Lower your voice, Marguerite, the entire band is listening to your drivel. In any event we must get started."

She no more wanted to hear me than I her. All blood had left her face; her lipless mouth was a pit, the mouth of a gun. "In Guatemala, Arbenz lost, not you. You went elsewhere. On the peninsula there was a victory. Not for you, you were a foreigner, admired, but without power. Algiers, likewise. The Congo—it was a massacre, they died, not you. You went elsewhere. To this country, my country. Even if you were to win—unlikely possibility—Rojos would win, Buteo would win, I would win—but not you!" She stood so close her spit sprayed my bloodless face. No matter how hard I tried I could not control the violent trembling that shook me head to toe. "You're afraid," she said, "to challenge victory or defeat. You're a solitary runner, Cordes, running from yourself. Get out! My people have suffered too many defeats, we can do without those of Ramón Cordes."

In the clearing outside the leanto my band moved about quietly, all ears no doubt. They had heard it all before they'd volunteered to be led by me. She was staring at me, teeth clenched, ignoring my upraised fists. Hatred made her brave.

"Power, power, power, that's all you talk about, Marguerite. The cry of the impotent. I'll not stoop to personal power, will not demean myself, the cause is too great for that." I needed time to regroup my forces. But she pressed forward, again attacked.

"You speak like a child. The most grubby little student leader knows better than that. You're a fool, Cordes. A timid little fool at that. You'll get out, disband, that's an order from Rojos, from the party. Or we will destroy you."

She had pressed too hard, driven me to high ground, a terrain I knew best.

I smiled. And that was almost enough. She backed away, body abruptly limp. She'd shot her bolt, whatever there was of it. "You frigid little bitch. For years Rojos, the party, commanded the guns, became careless with them, profligate, elevated them until the guns became supreme. Now the guns command the party and the party lives by us." She retreated again to the cot, sat slumped, the wildness having totally fled from her face. "I'll do as I please. Rojos has become static, atrophied, half dead. Like you. Without the likes of me he perishes. Proof? You have brought supplies, guns. From whom? Rojos! Why? He orders us to disband and sends us ammunition. Why? Because he knows our open comradeship with death is precisely what gives the *movement* power. If we die, so what? In death we become invincible. Another defeat which draws us closer to victory. The movement's victory." Outside the leanto, I could hear my men begin to talk, laugh. I had spoken for them, and they were letting me know they had heard.

I was standing before Marguerite, looking down at her. She stood, quivering. Reached out and took my hand in hers, drew it to her lips, kissed it, placed her warm flushed face against my open palm. It was a sincere gesture, and I was moved. We were comrades. In turn I drew her head to mine and kissed her. There was a terrible sadness about her that touched me deeply, but that I could not then comprehend. I only held her more closely, more tenderly, as she kissed my eyes, my cheeks, my lips.

78

It was in this fashion that Marguerite and I made love.

"Rojos told me to inform you there is a mine in the foothills to the puna which has recently reopened. The men are dissatisfied with their conditions. A few comrades and admirers of Cordes are among them. Perhaps they will join you."

"He didn't have great belief in your persuasive powers, did he?"

"He is a revolutionary and so long as you fight he is committed to aiding you." I could not see her eyes, she was rummaging in her backpack, withdrew a hand-drawn map. "Buteo can lead you there with this. It is approximately ten hours from here. The guns and ammunition are for those who will join you. You misunderstand Rojos, he is a generous man."

Jealousy tweaked me. "You and he?"

She shook her head sadly, she was drenched with sadness. "Don't be foolish, Ramón."

I believed her. Rojos was without any discernible tenderness, besides he had even less interest than I in entanglements. We are an obsessed *Bruderschaft*, Rojos, Buteo, Marguerite, Theo, I.

"I have to leave," she said, slipping into the backpack. "I have a job."

"You?"

"One of my aristocratic friends obtained it for me with the minister of defense." She laughed, the sadness suddenly dispelled. "He has hopes that some day I will be his. Now Rojos knows the disposition of troops before the president does. They have sent out one hundred fifty soldiers to find your band. Of course they don't know it is you. I was just talking. Is it Cordes? Could it

79

be he? No, the rumor is he is in China. China? The CIA has informed us he is in India. So it goes. Incidentally, killing that soldier last week was a stupidity."

"Delgado. He couldn't help himself. The soldier caught him literally with his pants down off the side of a road. A bad stomach. We all have a touch of it. The soldier almost passed with a wave of the hand, then saw Delgado's gun in his lap. Raised his own. Delgado shot him. Luckily the soldier brought up the rear of the patrol. By the time the others came running, Delgado was gone. We could have destroyed the entire patrol, nine men, if necessary, but they did not stay around long, were too frightened. It was bad luck. We left the area quickly. Delgado has been miserable."

She turned to leave my shelter. She was her old self—riding jeans, bulky jacket, backpack, yet that ridiculous slink, that leaning tower, that Pigalle pussy. "Shall I kiss you before I leave?"

"What for?"

"You're a bastard."

"No doubt. Armas will take you to the Portal. He's only twenty—the age which never tires and never satisfies. Be kind to him."

"Stop it, Ramón!"

"You're like a Norteamericano revolutionary, Marquerite. Overripe with promise, green sour at the core."

She seemed to shrink into herself, her pointed fawn's face wrinkled with pain from the pelting buckshot. She escaped from the leanto, I calmly at her skittering heels. The eyes of twenty men revived her with a shocking quickness. They were sitting around a small clearing, in pairs, singly, drinking hot coffee that Luis had made on the portable propane range, an efficient Abercrombie and Fitch appliance that no respectable guerrilla band could exist without. It was guaranteed not to smoke, therefore was undetectable from even the shortest distance. Marguerite sashayed, slunk, leaned lightly among them, her eyes beatific, her smile enigmatic. They knew her, of course. One man she touched with her elbow, another with an outstretched finger, still another she brushed with the sleeve of her jacket, one she kissed, Buteo, who ruffled her hair, smiled into another's eyes. Without saying a word, without moving, they became aroused, responded to her, began to crowd her, twenty men, she in the center, her lips wet, her eyes sparkling, her hips swaying, slinking, leaning more and more, her eyes wide, excited, theirs ruthless, harsh, grasping, so that soon, wordlessly, motionless, they pounced upon her, singly, in pairs, collectively. By the time she reached her horse, her eyes were glazed, her cheeks bloodred, her lips swollen. It could not have taken more than ten seconds.

When I approached her and Armas, she was still trembling and he ready for another go.

She reined in her horse, Armas had gone up ahead, and I wished her well. The past minute had vanished. That was Marguerite. She sat the horse simply, straightbacked, with dignity. I stared up into her face. It was her very own. That tender fawnlike beauty, wild, unreachable, her huge eyes filled with that mysterious sadness.

Impulsively I said, "Why don't you stay with us, Marguerite? Stay with us!"

Her head snapped back as if stunned, her eyes wild, pointed face white, and a stifled woeful cry escaped from her lips. Before I could say a word, she kicked her horse with her heels and went off at a gallop.

. .

I see her there, a sinuous black line against the stark blue of morning, her chestnut's tail whisking the flies, Armas square, jaunty on the white mare. He would lead her to the Portal in the mountains and rejoin us before we approached the mine.

The band and I decamped, donkeys weighed down with our supplies. The morning was brisk, the meadow grass crystalline with the early day's dew. Buteo and Rodolfo had gone ahead, our eyes and ears. We followed single file, silent, each bemused by the vastness of the day, each no doubt concerned with the news Marguerite had brought. I had put Rojos' demand that we disperse and leave the country to them directly and they had given their answer. We would close the mine, begin to harass the countryside, burn and pillage if necessary, and in the end destroy the government even if it took us years. Who could measure us, gauge us? We were as vagarious as the wind.

We marched for three hours, the morning's frost having slowly disintegrated under the rising sun. Rested. Ate tinned beef and bread, drank wine. Several, two North Americans, for whom it seemed to be endemic, and the Cuban, crawled off in solitude to relieve their angry, irritated intestines. I extracted my notebook from my shirt pocket and noted their emergency withdrawal. Every detail mattered. The band was small and had to be tended, nurtured, understood as one would a team of aerial artistes. One hand faltered, everyone broke his neck. Or hers. There were three women in the band. In this case, "I shit my brains out," could easily become, "I'll shoot your brains out." Thieves quarrel, thefts discovered. I laughed. Wrote again in the notebook: "It is permissible for a revolutionary to be witty, since to be witty is to barter in half-truths. But to be comic is fatal—for then one sees oneself, and the world, in a true light. It is impossible to remain obsessed—and without obsession there is nothing—if one can really laugh. Or cry." I raised my pen but did not stop thinking. Laughter and tears are universal and democratic, therefore counterrevolutionary. For a reason beyond my knowledge and for which I cannot account, Schleimann's single violent eye pierced my heart. Why at this particular moment? If laughter and tears are counterrevolutionary, then what about love and conscience?

Enough! Laughter, tears, conscience, love shall have to abide their time. I raised my hand to signal Max, the Argentinian, to start the band moving. He stood, a tall man, a giant, a quiet, graceful man with a quick intelligence. We knew and understood each other well. I had but to think and he would know. His orders were laconic, to the point. He respected the members of the band and they respected him. If a man shirked, Max merely stared at him. The man immediately responded. Max loved power, but only as second in command. He would be a general loyal to the ruler. But if the ruler misruled, Max would kill him and find another. After the seizure of power, others would disappear, defect, be shot, Max would survive. Still, a contradiction, he was the kind of animal who dies in captivity. He was a son of the working class. His father had been an authoritarian trade union leader. He was a revolutionary.

As they began to clamber to their feet I observed them. Every one of them was young, alert, strong, constant and totally committed to my leadership. Even Delgado, the former Cuban pickpocket and brothel exhibitionist, whose conversion to our cause had been swift, his passion that of a warlike monk. They understood it was exactly my alleged weakness, my inability to engage in combat for personal power, that protected them against being wasted by virtue of my own vanity. My band believed as I did, that the commune can only be founded on an escape from individuality. Their individuality. Not mine. I am an elitist cadre. Still, they knew I would yield my life as readily as theirs. It is the clash of truths which provokes progress. Contradictions detonate revolutions. There were, as I said, three women in the band, young, solemn, durable. If there was sexual interplay, it was secret, private. No jealousy, envy, had disrupted one moment of the band's life. No rules had ever been laid down; no discussion held. The band was a true collective, voluntary. Their discipline was self-imposed. What one did in the secrecy of one's bedroll was one's own affair—so long as the life of the commune remained unscathed. As they rose to their feet one face emerged—the face of the band. Determined, stalwart, obsessive, compulsive, fanatic. The band would surround the mine, destroy it and everyone but those who would join us. The laughter would die in the glutted throat of the capital city, and Rojos would understand his day had come and vanished. Even a tortoise must one day die.

As the band marched single file behind me, one man separated himself from the others and went ahead, our advance guard, our eyes, our ears: Buteo, the peasant's son, the native of this land, who had in the two months of our campaign succeeded, as I had hoped he would, in elevating himself above the mass. It was now certain he would assume leadership of this country after the revolution was won.

And I? What seas would I sail? Which governments would topple? That of my own country? I remembered Marguerite's words—". . . what is there that frightenes you so?" My old ones, my brothers and sisters . . . why do I attempt to answer? To answer is to admit that my motives are psychological, subjective, a passive response to accidental stimuli, rather than an act of intellectual will to formulate ideology, to command history. A heresy. Full of heresies today. March! Plan the oncoming assault.

We climbed the foothills quietly, cautious yet swift. Personal meanderings were of no importance. Only the mine had meaning. Its darkness, its tunnels cut deep into the earth, its ore, its iron cars, its pickaxes, shovels, its shoring timbers, its rats, its men who stooped and crawled, hacking at its flesh with broken fingernails, sweat-grimed faces. And its guards. I remembered that Marguerite had neglected to tell me how many men guarded the mine. Or was it that I had neglected to ask? Another detail forgotten. The specific lost for the general. That has always been my way. Details, specifics are for clerks. No matter. Buteo and his aide, Rodolfo, will reach the mine long before us and will report what they have seen.

The valley was below us, already in shadow, when Rodolfo's smiling features greeted me from between two colo trees. His approach had been so silent I had not been aware of his presence until then. He was twenty-two, slight, with quick, nervous hands and a long humorous face which he kept cleanly shaven. He wanted to be easily read. When he spoke the tip of his long nose kept time with the tempo of his words. Usually he spoke rapidly, in a high alto chirp. His childhood had been tragic, having lost his entire immediate family to an oceanic tidal wave on the South American coast when he was ten. He bartered a jester's cheerfulness for affection.

"You've been slow today, Ramón. Have you been out hunting lizards?"

"Out with it, Rodolfo."

"Buteo's still observing. It will be sport. Two lazy guards with carbines." His nose was beating a fast tune. "Very little activity outside the mine, though there seem to be many men inside and out. Oh, yes, a half hour from here. Buteo suggests the band camp here for the night and attack early in the morning before they can wipe the phlegm out of their eyes and take a long piss. Have you ever gone into battle with a full bladder? Aieee."

I gave him the laughter he worked so hard to earn. "Anything else, Rodolfo?"

"No, Ramón. May I return now? Buteo wishes me to remain at our observation post during the night so he can return to plan the battle." He was off before I concluded my assenting nod.

"Rodolfo," I called after him, "no fire, and not one shot unless as a danger signal to us."

"I understand. Buteo has already warned me. I will kill my quota in the morning," and he smiled charmingly at me before he disappeared into the brush.

When I turned, the entire band had already vanished into the trees to make camp for the night, to unroll their blankets, to unlace their shoes, to freshen themselves with water from canteens. The guards were set. Luis had the propane stove going, preparing hot soup. The pack horses and donkeys were tethered. Zena, the Canadian, had been sent by Max to await Armas's return from the Portal at a set compass point a mile behind us.

Except for Luis and myself, the forest was as it had always been, the whispering of trees, the hiss of insects, the flutter of wings. Now I heard Luis's wooden ladle on the big iron pot.

I found myself a likely tree, an aromatic cedar, unrolled my bag, made camp.

And awaited Buteo.

X ───────────────

We fly along the edge of the puna until the bay is drenched with sweat, her sensitive mouth with lather. She is breathing heavily and I must rein her in, I must be kind to her, she has given me yeoman service. The two riderless horses are wet but breathing easily. I dismount and lead the three horses to the shade of a skimpy yareta to rest for a few moments. I have discerned no movement in the distance and I begin to wonder about my comrades. Conclude they are being overly cautious and are proceeding toward me through the trees that stretch from the lower foothills of the mountains easterly across the puna.

The strong wine I had obtained from the shepherdess refreshes me, invigorates me, reinvests me with joy. I am filled with regret that I had not been bolder and had not drunk from her, rested my head between her breasts, slid my hand along the silken skin of her inner thigh. We shall meet again, I am certain, this time as lovers, not strangers, and I marvel at the suddenness of my love for her and hers for me, thinking simultaneously it is a mirage or the fulfillment of a profound yearning. It is not she or I, it is the propitious time for love for both of us, for her, the first love after the early love of her old ones, the awaited love of story and fable, for me, the arrival point of love after the many encounters. For the moment I understand the time has come for my assumption of power and that after we have won here and someone, perhaps one among those approaching me— not Buteo, stolid, strong Buteo, he is dead—has been enthroned, I shall return to my own land with the shepherdess as my wife and comrade. Buteo is dead. I am certain he is dead, for I can see, more, feel, his patient, cruel eyes upon me as his blood courses, darkening the slag of the mine.

I snap the clasp of the image, withdraw an old shirt from my rucksack and begin to wipe the bay mare down, to dry her. She leans ever so lightly against me, nuzzles me playfully with her head, to show me her affection, and I whisper my own in return. I stop. Stare about. My hand trembles. What was that I heard? Listen. A whimper. A strange sigh; a stifled sob. It is near. Silence. But the mare's ears stiffen, quiver, she too has heard. There it is again. A harrowing whimper. I suppress my own cry, turn an ear to listen. Again. It comes from the far side of the yareta where the moss-like foliage is denser. The horses are prancing about nervously, snorting through quivering nostrils, frightened. I speak loudly to them, reassuringly, "It is nothing, old nags, be at ease, nothing," as I draw my knife and begin slowly, quietly to circumnavigate the perimeter of the bush. A strange, wide-girthed bush, it emits a strong swamp odor, for where I have dismounted it is dying, its mossy leaves desiccated, yet as I make a turn it is rich, heavy, so it is only half-dead, dying, the odor of death upon it, sour-sweet, fetid. Giving refuge to a crippled wild beast, no doubt, at its most violent time. Involuntarily I cough and my mouth is filled with my own sour-sweetness, and I spit a gob of blood, which glistens like an evil jewel on the green ichu grass. At the following turn of the bush there is a gasp and, my hand with the knife outflung, I leap into the open, away from the yareta. Stare wildly. For an old man clothed in rags, his swart face deeply furrowed, yellowing, his eyes like burnt-out pits, is sitting cross-legged on the earth, cradling in his brittle, blackened, bony hands a rigid bundle of tattered cloth from which protrudes a woman's gray wizened face. From his eyes tears fall. She is dead.

Sheathing my knife, mournfully I approach them. Speak to the old man, but though he hears me, lifts those burnt-out eyes to me, he does not answer, perhaps does not understand. But he raises his quavery hands to me, asking me to help him. I kneel, and with gentle hands remove the weight of his old dead wife, and she is a withered leaf, then grasp his hands and help him unbend his stiff, fragile bones until he stands, and he is a dried-out bough who reaches to my shoulders.

Greedily, he drinks the wine I offer, eats a crumble of cheese, a few berries, the soft center of bread. She who was once comely lies on the earth curled like a foetus, gray, dead. Buried, it will not be long before she is dust.

I again speak to the old man but he merely stares at me with his bottomless eyes, his toothless mouth pursed, as though safekeeping the words. What is there to say?

From my rucksack I fetch the small, sharp shovel with the folding handle, a cunning affair, and begin to dig a grave. The old man stays my hand, his fingers are two crook'd bones, shaking his head. Turning up the palms of my hands, hunching my shoulders, I ask, "What is it you want from me?" He points to the horses. Yes, I understand. Entwined a lifetime, having drunk from the same stream, the same cup, having been couched on a single bed, her soft belly, his calloused hands, eking life from the same earth, he cannot leave her now. He wishes to take her on a journey.

The saddle removed, merely the sheepskin blanket remaining, the old man sits atop the chestnut gelding with the white markings on forelegs and head, a huge, strong horse with a thick neck and sly eyes like a spoiled child, and he sits her well, the reins light in his old, gnarled fingers. Before him on the chestnut's thick neck I strap his dead wife, first securing the tattered skirt about her legs so that in death her dignity will not be offended. His pockets I stuff with cheese, bread, about his shoulders I hang my flask still half-filled with the shepherdess's tart wine. He opens the purse of his mouth, utters a few metallic sounds that I understand to be words of gratitude and farewell, lightly flicks the reins and departs.

I stand and watch him now. The bay mare and the sorrel gelding whinny loud, call after their departing friend. I caution them to remain silent. But the chestnut has heard, responds, pulls on the reins with his strong neck and I begin to doubt the old peasant can hold him. But the ancient one digs deeply into the almost forgotten past, discovers a reserved unused strength, he knows where he is going. The chestnut wavers, pulls, concedes. The old one is master of his fate.

He has turned into the foothills to the mountains. He will take his wife high into the mountains, to their very height, to the peaks capped with virgin snow. And there he will lie with her, staring with his burnt-out bottomless pits into the sun, and they will together resume their journey into ash.

Collect yourself! Move on! Your comrades, new fighters, sent by your friend are impatient to meet you. The revolution, history, waits. Hurry!

The bay mare has had her rest, I prefer her to the sorrel, remount, again join time, off in a gallop in the shadow now of the foothills along the edge of the puna. In the distance, among the trees, there is a familiar burst of shots. I count. One, two . . . three. Another burst. One, two . . . three. *Come.* They have made camp and await my arrival. A new band, an old struggle. Faces change, never history.

Today it might very well be Tupac who was born on the altoplana as a few days before it was Buteo; where Tupac is stolid and slow, Buteo was stolid and quick. He had the swiftest hands I have ever seen. Perhaps it was an illusion, a *trompe-l'oeil*, a normal quickness made to seem quicker in contrast to the slow speech, cautious exercise of his body. When he rejoined us in the heights above the mine, we had already eaten, set the guard, fanned, and faded out into the bush, so that he stood for a moment in the small clearing wondering if he had perhaps lost his way. He beetled his black brows, nibbled a lip, searched impatiently about. At the count of five we stepped forward, encircling him, and in mock fear he flung his powerful arms high above his head and cried, "I surrender, I surrender," and we laughed, as if we were playing at soldiers and thieves.

As we seated ourselves around him to hear his report

on the mine, I remember wondering whether the serious game we played was not as childish. Merely for a flashing moment. I refuse to believe that life is absurd. I am not Hamlet, alas, I am Ramón Cordes.

We sat under a new moon at first quarter.

"Proceed, Buteo," I said.

He stood in the center of the circle slowly turning as he spoke so that all shared him equally. He stood and spoke with assurance, at ease, and I could not repress the smile which turned my lips. On the peninsula he had been a good comrade, quick with his gun, quick to follow a command, but shy, quiet, close-mouthed, ill at ease with himself, with his leaders, his comrades—perhaps it could be said not at home with his surroundings. Still, he had been as obsessed as everyone else with the revolution—but—but it had not been his own. As quick to risk his life as any—still to him it had not been life or death. Now, transported a few thousand miles to his own country, after sixty days of repeated failure, he stood before us rooted in the earth, this is my land, I am at home with it and myself, and it is to me all or nothing. And those sitting around him, listening intently, acknowledged it, accepted it, expected it. If we won in this land, it would be his to rule, to govern, to command, to direct, to destroy and to resurrect. But until that moment of ascension, it was Ramón Cordes who was the arbiter of history, the comander. I listened.

"In the few hours I observed the mine I counted fifty men entering and leaving. There are probably many more inside, for it is one of the very deep mines . . ."

Theo, our ideologue, interrupted, "What do they mine?"

Buteo smiled. "Silver. It might very well be the richest silver mine in the world, though my people are among the poorest."

"The miners ought then be even more willing to join us," Theo said. And the band nodded assent. It seemed a most rational conclusion, though I knew it was not. Too simple. Men join the revolution only when they have severed ties with the past. The more complete the schism, the more total the revolutionary. Even among the twenty-three of the band there were several to whom it was only a game of chance, though they played it seriously, compulsively, to the death—the stake only themselves; and one was a low-life thief. Cordes, the revolution, could hardly care less—he, it, used anyone so long as he or she carried a gun with intent to kill. Ideologically it was understood the adventurers, the thief, would be used recklessly, would be, hopefully, the first to die.

Buteo was speaking, describing in detail what he had observed, and I was distracted, not listening, eyes on the twinkling Archer in the starlit night, and perhaps that is why I did not give more serious thought, did not give any thought to the number of uniformed men with guns he had counted. Eight guns. To guard what might well be the richest silver lode in the world? Not one of the band questioned it, but of course it was up to me, and I did not. I was counting the stars. It could be several of the band did think about it, but, not hearing a word from me, their leader, decided it might not have importance. So it is with a crowd, a mass, an army, a guerrilla band. In the subsequent discussion, we spoke of every possibility, every probability, before we decided on a course of action. We desired to win, not lose. Yet we did not discuss the obvious: eight guards with guns to protect the silver mine when it was known a guerrilla band operated in the area? That passed us by. Not a word. I measured the universe.

Thought of immortality . . .

I permitted Buteo to lead the discussion. He was patient, assured, without passion, intelligent, a veteran of many assaults. I was not envious of his rise to leadership. Why should I have been? I had wound the clock, flicked the pendulum. It swung, steady on course; the clock ticked in perfect time. He did not challenge me, he accorded me respect and treated me with great correctness. He had accepted the challenge to himself from himself—he understood instinctively the power was his to win or lose. I was satisfied. Indeed, happy. There rested my immortality. I am not Dzugashvili, so replete with vanity and envy that I cannot bear the thought of sharing immortality with my peers and so seek to destroy them in life. False vanity, demeaning envy. If my peers attain immortality, I shall sit among them in the throne room of heaven, if for no other reason than that we shared the same time and space on earth.

These were the thoughts which turned my eyes to the stars the evening before our assault on the mine. There was no act or word, no uttered thought from myself or anyone that could have prepared me for what was to follow in that purple-gray killing hour which hovers between dawn and day.

As we talked, we cleaned and oiled our guns. One of my innovations. Examined carelessly it can be thought to be superficial; examined closely it can be seen to be profound. To an assault, the gun is central. No gun, no assault. Obvious. If we discuss the positions we are to take, the concealment, the tentative forward movement of one segment of our band, the probe by another, the sly withdrawal, the testing, the infiltration, the further probing, the surge, the powerful plunge, the naked assault—with the gun lying aside, a separate entity, it all appears academic. It is a textbook discussion. Almost sterile. When the actual attack is launched, the gun is merely an adjunct, a piece of metal bolted to a stock of wood whose purpose it is to perform a purely mechanical function. It is an added weight one has a momentary impulse to fling aside. But to clean the gun, oil its parts, polish, yes, fondle them, during the foreplay, so to speak, then it becomes wholly identified with the assault, is integral to it, at the heart of it. The gun is the attack as you are the attack. It is your arm, your hand, your claw—more, it is your secret violence. That is why professional soldiers, professional killers, sleep with their gun, learn to love it, respect it, protect it, polish it, nurture it, cradle it close to their . . . I am carried away and have revealed an intimacy that embarrasses me. A gun is merely a gun. It shoots and it kills, why do I become sentimental about it? I answer myself: to conceal the cruelty with which you have so frequently used it.

Decision seized unanimously.

Before the final roll call, I as the arbiter had asked our customary question. "If anyone dissents assert it now." It is an iron rule of guerrilla action, especially with small bands, as ours was, that no assault be launched with even one participating dissenter. If only unconsciously, a dissenter will lag in performance of duty. One lost moment can destroy the timing of the attack and victory will be lost. I asked the question. No one stood. Of course, there is unspoken group pressure —the cruelest, most oppressive—but it was assumed every member of the band was brave enough to face it. None stood. If anyone had he would have been assigned to tend our pack animals, after all, someone must. But, dissenting, victory would not be his. Still, neither would the defeat. The possibility exists. No one stood. One there must have been, there always is. No one stood. Was he or she thinking perhaps of the future? *Of that time when we would rule and the purges would begin?* "At the historic taking of the mine, the turning point in Cordes's guerrilla compaign, Alonzo lost faith in the revolution and stood aside as he now stands aside when we must destroy the enemies of the people . . ." A powerful revolutionary weapon. Perhaps the most powerful among our adherents, especially now that every year finds more countries in our camp. Soon the world shall be ruled unanimously, left and right clasping hands. No one stood. I smiled and wished them a good night's rest.

We dispersed in the darkness to attempt sleep for a few hours, though for most of us the excitement and the fear would make sleep impossible. A few, the fortunate ones, would discover the haven of sleep before their heads touched the ground. That is not because they are braver or have less fear but because at least in this regard their nervous systems are healthier, that is, have a stronger thrust for self-preservation. If they did not sleep they would go mad. Yet, when the enemy was engaged, they would be no less or no more brave than anyone else. An unimportant generalization.

I sent new guards to replace the old, who, upon their return, were advised of our decisions. It was too late for them to demur, and they did not—a sacrifice, it is true, but one they accepted without question. They retired. As I sat in my lair under the cedar with Buteo, a new Buteo, no longer self-effacing, shy, but strong, forceful, assured, a guard led Armas, who had just returned with Zena, to us and left. Zena would be instructed by Max. She was a Canadian, slender, yet heavy at breast and thigh, with a solemn, intelligent face, fair-skinned, engaging in a serious way. She rarely if ever laughed. Quoted Lenin for every problem. If she had a lover in the band, none but he knew. Her privacy was her own. She never for a moment doubted she was any man's equal, therefore no man ever doubted it as well. Fierce, determined, warlike, she had a steady hand and a sharp eye. Zena would join Buteo in the first charge.

Buteo asked Armas to sit with us, gave him a tin of cold beef and a slab of bread which the boy gobbled quickly, downing the food with long draughts of wine. He was the youngest in the band, a strong, stocky boy with a dark taciturn face, intelligent, one of Buteo's countrymen. At one point he turned to me as if to speak, but thought better of it, concentrated on the bread, chewing it loudly. A diffident boy, I felt I should help him.

"How did the trip with Marguerite go, Armas?"

He swallowed heavily, hesitated, then spoke. "At the Portal when we said goodbye she was very nervous, strange." He looked away.

"Marguerite? In what way?" I asked, raising an eyebrow.

"Oh, I don't know, jumpy." He shrugged and continued eating.

"Try to be specific, Armas. It must have been something unusual for it to disturb you."

The boy stopped chewing, thought a moment, as if trying to find the right words. "It's difficult to say exactly. She just acted as if she didn't want to leave . . . Unhappy, upset, I guess. Yes. She looked the way you do when you lose your nerve. I suppose she was worried about us." He took a long swig of wine.

"It's Rojos," I said to him and Buteo. "He's lost *his* nerve. To her, you know, he's a stone god."

"All he is is a hard turd," Buteo said. And the three of us laughed.

When he had concluded eating, Armas asked, "What are the decisions?" When it concerned our work, he was not shy, he was, in fact, aggressive, arrogant, and already showed elitist qualities.

"Buteo will tell you."

They stood. "Come with me to the observation post," Buteo said. "Rodolfo should be relieved. I'll explain our plans as we go."

"We will join you there at four-thirty," I reminded him. "Meanwhile I'll try to snatch some sleep."

My friend smiled affectionately. "If you get some sleep, Ramón, it will mean your time has come to be put out to pasture." Is it the wish or the thought which is husband to the other—or are they so long married they have become indistinguishable? As he left with Armas I could hear him say, "That man never sleeps and never seems to be the tireder for it." They disappeared silently into the whispering darkness under the trees and I stretched out on my sleeping bag, my gun a pleasant weight at my side. I heard a twig snap in the direction they had taken and I sat up with a start as Buteo's broad form emerged alone, his gun swinging loosely at his side.

"What goes, old friend?" I said.

He said nothing, merely approached me in a slow stroll, his shadow huge from the quarter moon. I regarded him quizzically—what was he about?—when he dropped to his knee at my side, took my hand in his, and clasped it warmly. And was gone.

I turned to my side, closed my eyes, heard the birds calling, whistling, cawing. What Buteo had said about my sleeping habits was not completely true, for I immediately fell asleep. For an hour. A truly deep, pure sleep. I knew little fear. I had been in many assaults, and it appeared this one would be among the simplest.

When I awoke, I threaded my way in the darkness among the trees to a brook earlier discovered by one of our men, fell to my knees and repeatedly plunged my head into the glacial water until I was totally awake.

As I sat with my back against the cedar tree—my favorite posture of repose—I began to review our discussion and our plan of attack. The night air was quiet and wore a frostlike chill. A good hundred yards away I heard an owl's dying screech slice through a woodpecker's thumping on a hollow tree. I heard several men—the fortunate ones—snore, but mostly I could hear men endlessly muttering, cursing. Simultaneously they wished for the night never to end and for it to end immediately. In the interval between the decision seized and the assault there is too much time for thought; in battle, too little. All we know is that when another man falls—enemy or friend—we feel a little better. We have survived him. When the battle terminates, we count the dead. The more dead, the better we feel. We have survived the many. We, the survivors, are the chosen. We do not cogitate long on the thought. It is an instinctive reaction, one that we fear but solely because we know that some day we shall be among the many.

As I sat with my back against the living tree I thought about Buteo. His clasp was still warm upon my hand. Gratitude or affection? Perhaps both. I smiled. Coldly.

He had insisted during the band's discussion that he lead the initial charge. We had demurred. But his arguments were cogent. The miners would respect him more, thus be more amenable to his persuasion. He spoke their language, was a countryman. I pointed out that his argument had validity, but was too simple. Sentimental. He looked at me sharply. Then I smiled coldly, too. He had, I said, become a leader and leaders must survive; they were not articles of manufacture, they rose from within themselves and the historical circumstance; on the peninsula I had led the charges and our loyal friend had taken up the rear since it had been most necessary that he survive.

"Exactly," Buteo said, himself smiling.

I could then have said that I had no intention of leading the charge, that Max was the logical choice, Max and Armas; Buteo, Theo and I could take up the rear. But I held my tongue. Buteo had not yet matured into supreme leadership. A romantic still, he played with death. It dulled his mind, the alternative neither appeared nor appealed to him. If there were a choice, he must die and I must live. The leader must survive, he must count the dead.

On the peninsula, I had led the assaults, had risked death most and our friend and leader had risked it least. If we won, who would rule? We had accepted it as an historical law—more, as a law of nature. Still, men are men. After victory, there had been snickers, contemptuous little smiles, snide asides. Unfair, romantic, but there it was. Buteo could risk death, but he could not risk that. His instinct for dominance, leadership, survival had not yet ripened to full fruition. Immature.

The band understood it instinctively, I consciously—after all, I had dwelt in that orchard for quite some time—and it had been decided that Buteo would lead the charge. Theo, the ideologue, Armas, a native of this country and, though young, a man with elitist potential, and Cordes would take up the rear.

Blind, cruel, sweet Buteo exulted.

And, unreasonably, unasked, unwilled, for the first time I tasted the wretched bitter fruit of envy. And fear. Full power over my survival had been thrust into my unwilling hands.

The sky illuminating the mine camp was gray striated with dark purple and red layers of light from an unseen unleavened sun. At our observation point it was still night black, the trees dripping dew with a sharp coldness on our faces and hands. Below, the mine camp lay sprawled like an unsightly, clumsy, sleepy beast—a rump of rickety wooden barracks, heaps of slag, narrow gauge tracks like a gleaming spine running its length to a huge black maw in the sheer face of the mountain. Two guards with carbines stood at the mouth to the mine shaft. Four miners sat on their heels in front of the barracks drinking from tin mugs. To the left of the tracks, midway up between the barracks and the shaft, two additional guards slouched on either side of a door to a small adobe structure from the windows of which shone a yellow light. No other life. Lying about in predawn disuse were pickaxes, an old North American jeep, and on the tracks which ran from the shaft through the heaps of slag to somewhere around the barracks sat four miniature freight cars commonly called donkeys by miners. Behind me the band stood expectant, coiled.

I lowered the binoculars, captured Buteo's eye, and nodded. He and I embraced, as did many others. Several kissed. Everyone managed to touch, to feel, to impart comradeship and love to at least one other, then, smiling at Theo, Armas and me, the remainder of the band began their descent. According to our charts, the sun would rise above the horizon in fifteen minutes. At that point, the three of us would open fire—Armas at the guards to the adobe hut, apparently the office, I at those who guarded the mine shaft, and Theo at those guards who might show themselves at the barracks. In fifteen minutes those guards would be dead. Armas and I were certain of that. From this distance they were blank faces. Four mannequins in uniform carrying guns. Riddled with bullets, sawdust would fly. Their eyes would never corrupt my sleep.

After we began our fire, Buteo, leading Delgado, Zena, Rodolfo and seven others, would slip from the woods that surrounded the mine camp in a large irregular semicircle, and utilizing the heaps of slag and the rusty iron donkeys as cover, open full fire and charge on the opening of the shaft which lay to our left. A few seconds afterward, Max and his squad of eight would begin their assault on the barracks to the right. At the observation post on the heights we would assert a ceaseless covering fire.

The submachine guns in the competent hands of the

103

band were vastly superior—five-to-one in fire power at the least—to the carbines held by the guards. The possibility existed that there were several guards who had not been observed by Buteo and Rodolfo. The miners, we were certain, would not fight. They were militant syndicalists among whom were comrades who waited to join us. Buteo's mission was to close the mine shaft to prevent any guards inside from joining the defenders; that of Max, likewise, at the barracks. The adobe hut was to be covered by the two men of each squad closest to each other.

All the guards would be killed; miners only if they fought against us. In this way would the miners know that we were not involved in a sporting event, with silver as the trophy. Our essential interest was the miners. Unless a guerrilla band grows, it must begin to disintegrate. This is crucial to all guerrilla operations. Once it begins to grow, it must continue to proliferate, and so long as it does victories are common. And, again, as victories increase, the band increases. Soon the process is irreversible. The band becomes an army; an army the people; the people a government. Since its inception, not one native of the country had joined the band. From what Marguerite had told me and from what I now observed with my naked eye, it appeared likely our fortunes were about to change. To use Trotsky's phrase, the leaping transformation . . .

Theo, Armas and I attended. Under the trees the night-black darkness became gray-green. At the mine there was little movement. The four miners continued to drink from their metal mugs, chatted; the guards guarded. The band descended silently, an occasional leaf shook, a bough. Far beyond the valley, the sun like a fiery gold octopus began its swarm into a magenta heaven. Young Armas, slumped calmly over his gun, maintained a beetle-browed, dark-eyed confrontation with his watch. In fifteen minutes his back would straighten, his hands would raise the gun, his finger would flick and the two guards at the adobe hut would be dead. I smiled at him with fraternal affection; he caught it from the corner of his eye and winked. The gaunt, Gallic face of Theo, still young at thirty, was set in a stony harshness—all pretend, for this was his first battle, and he was a sensitive, delicate soul who would soon learn that the ideological enemy bled and screamed from a very human larynx, and inwardly he would weep, I knew. Yes, Theo, who on paper had written the bold staggering words: *We must kill the killers!*

I close my eyes and hear the same old song . . .

The second hand seemed to have all the time in the world. Wild macaws and cuckoos screamed. And the mind of Ramón Cordes wandered through the winding corridors between closed and opened doors, among storied tapestries and secret, heavy folded drapes that led inevitably to Marguerite. There must have been some inner intelligence, some intuitive force that led me now as the second hand took its infernal time to her. My engine of destruction. My cornucopia of contradictions. Unliberated, passionate, frigid revolutionary. Why had I in my wanderings at any time been compelled to stop at her door? There had been Deborah, Erica, Annette— all liberated, intelligent, rational women, comely too, who could have given me (and what I them?) love compounded with generosity. No. Marguerite. Fiercely moved to obtain justice for her people, she coiled to leap —again the leaping transformation—lost nerve in midstride. Hysterical, she straddled the chasm, one foot in the past, one in the future. Stared into the abyss, lost balance, clutched at Rojos. Tortoises do not leap. They crawl. Rojos's orthodoxy was her straitjacket, her survival kit. And Rojos knew, he was if nothing canny, and used her like a weapon.

Wandering, thinking, I could feel myself become tense. The second hand moved faster. What was it? There was a drumming in my temples. The macaws screeched. A hawk plunged. Armas sat calmly, Theo clenched his Gascon jaw. She had come in her little red Lancia bearing gifts—guns, ammo, herself, information about the mine. Miner comrades working at the mine. Yet, also, Ramón, desist, disband, Rojos believes you are doing injury to his—our—revolution.

Rojos was my counterpart—separated by a generation. He was no less obsessed and no less cruel, he too had a single way that he must go. Ramón's a foreigner, not one of us. She herself had told me. After Delgado's unfortunate killing of a soldier, they had sent one hundred fifty troops to find my band . . . reopened a rich silver mine with but eight men to guard it. There it was down below!

The second hand ran like a madman.

I stood.

Armas called, "Still time. Five minutes."

I barely heard him. My thoughts were among the corridors. He would not dare. She would not comply. Yes, she would. She had concealed her petty self for all the years of her life, and then, in weakness, had revealed herself to me. I knew what she had most wished to hide. Yes, she would. And he would dare. Wouldn't I? Loyalty . . . to him—and me—a hoax to cruelly trap the tender. It was not for nothing that he was called Pizarro and I Cortés.

The sporty little red Lancia had led the way.

Below, in a few moments, my band was going to its certain death. From behind us I was certain we three were being watched. Ramón Cordes, wizard at seeing the invisible, had been blind to the obvious. Eyes, eyes were all about us. I can never escape the eyes. Ramón Cordes. One of the elite. History, personal circumstances, accident and individual will produced me. How many do we number in the world? Speak to the computers. Read history. I say, READ HISTORY!

Armas sang out clearly for the entire world to hear him, "Two minutes."

If I were mistaken, the band would have no difficulty from the guards without our covering fire. If not, it would make no difference. Quietly, calmly, I said, "Don't change your positions. Keep cool, I have something to tell you. We are being watched." Imperceptibly they tensed. "At three seconds make a break for the trees. They will follow. Armas, you will take cover and hold them off, Theo and I will go down to the mine. Every bullet will count."

Our break was clean. Those observing us were caught dumb—it took a good second and a half before they shot their first round. Bullets tore overhead, but we made the trees. Armas ducked behind a thick black walnut; Theo and I kept going downhill. More carbine shots. Then I heard Armas's gun infinitely faster, and his loud, strong laugh.

I ran heedless to Theo, to the branches tearing at my body, my head, only shielding my eyes with an arm. Firing continued behind me, below the battle was joined.

Our guns were distinctive, rapid, sharp, then one loud continuous roar. The response of the carbines was desultory, snappish. For a brief time our fire outweighed the enemy's and as I tore madly down the mountainside I began to wonder if the band would perform a miracle, elude the trap, and gain a victory.

Abruptly the answering fire became heavier, equaled ours. But then Max and his squad joined their guns to the battle and again the fire power was ours. I ran swifter, heartened, hopeful, yet wondered, for the enemy had not committed more than twenty guns. Where were the rest? Again as if in answer, I heard the carbine fire increase. Forty, fifty guns. Still we maintained equality, perhaps slight superiority. The firing was incessant. Then the duller report of carbines ceased. Only the sharper, more rapid firing of our guns could be heard. Inexhaustible, exuberant with rage, I approached the mine camp and could see open space from among the trees and brush. Only my comrades were shooting, a torrent, a tidal wave. I could not believe my ears. Had we won? Where was the bulk of the enemy guns? I had but a few steps to take to the clearing, was yet slightly above it, concealed by brush, when I saw—no! not yet! —Zena's solemn, fair head rising above the heaps of slag, followed by Delgado's, others, smiling, happy.

Then from my left, shattering the dawning sky, thundered volley after volley from the phalanx of a hundred guns. Zena broke in two. Delgado exhibited his flesh.

Dazed, I stood, encompassing disaster, until the entire mine camp sprawled silent before my stricken eyes. It was an arena surrounded by wooded hills and the mountainside which housed the mine itself. A dense lavender haze of dust and refracted prismatic light hovered about the silence. From just above the trees to the east the sky slanted reddish gold and blue.

Nothing moved. Absolute silence. Not an echo.

A few feet before me, in the clearing, lay the giant body of Max, arms outflung, blood still pouring from his mouth and eyes. At his right sat Robert, the black Brazilian poet, leaning over his gun as if taking careful aim. He was insolently dead. Charles, the loquacious North American addict whom we had cured with our comradeship, lay prone to the left of Max and behind a boulder, seemingly asleep. The guards at the opening of the mine curled grotesquely upon the earth; inside the mine others could be seen. The two guards at the door to the adobe hut had been hit in their chests, thrown backwards against the wall. They sat, chests medallioned with little red holes, their faces calm, their eyes glazed. Rodolfo lay on his back under a jeep, bartering a betrayed smile for its axle's affection. The four miner-soldiers we had observed drinking from tin mugs were exactly where we had seen them—guns, not mugs, clutched in hand, sprawled head to head like spokes in a wheel, death their hub. And from the heaps of slag sprouted my remaining dead, a sorry garden.

My eyes searched for Buteo's cruel, generous head.

Could not find it. Imperceptibly I moved to enter the arena—I must find him—but intelligence prevailed, and, instead, retreated a few steps. I was the leading cadre, must survive for other defeats and other victories.

As I turned my head the silence was ripped brutally from the sky. A hundred carbines emptied their clips into the slag. The dead must be made securely dead. I heard a barked command, then saw some eighty men step forward from a great stand of cedar on the hill directly opposite to where I stood. Guns on the ready, in battle formation, they approached the mining camp. He was a cautious commander, but the cautious are never cautious enough. If one of my men still lived many of the soldiers were going to die. I could have killed a goodly number myself before they hit the ground. But I was not about to reveal my existence. I lived and was not ready to die. Not yet.

But I could not break away. I wondered about Armas and Theo. They had not joined me. Probably had been killed.

The soldiers advanced, guns ready, entered the mine clearing, their commander in the fore. From among the slag heaps deathly silence. My gun was at my chest before I knew I had raised it. Again, the eternal struggle— emotion or intelligence; sentimentality or reason. Sentimentality had cost Buteo his life. That clasping hand of gratitude and affection because I had not ordered him to the rear and Max to command the assault. Sentimental men do not lead revolutions. He had no right to survive. I did not alter the command as I had intended. He lay inert and I survived. I held my fire. Advised myself to leave. But weakness held me. My eyes must view the dead.

The soldiers had now advanced into the clearing. Guns ready, eyes alert. The commander's taut face was about to relax in victory. From the slag heaps total silence. Death ruled. A sudden glint of metal! The commander threw himself to the ground. Called a command. A submachine gun flared into action. Soldiers scattered and fell like trees hit by a tornado. Only one gun could move so swiftly—Buteo's. For a brief moment, as my gun and heart leaped to him, I felt a stab of dismay. Was it because he lived or because my presence was now revealed to the enemy?

I stand and die as a man. I am no saint and no divinity.

It was too late, of course. Perhaps if I had shot earlier, the enemy taken by surprise, he might have made his escape. By now the enemy had found cover and threw down a ceaseless fire. I shot endless rounds, as did Buteo, until the sun had catapulted high over the horizon and fiercely assaulted the heavens. Buteo had no chance. I still did. His fire, his change of clips so fast, they dared not move. But he was lost and knew it. Their bullets turned the heap of slag before him into a piddling pile and dessicated the trees and brush about my head until they yielded little cover.

Finally he stood to take their collective aim—blood poured from his head. His eyes—eyes that I had known in quick succession to be generous, cruel, tender, obsessed—were as he fell cast in my direction. They were wide open as if trying for the last time to encompass the entire universe, asking, is all or any of it worth the cruelty and pain?

For a quick moment, animal that I am, I glanced at all my dead, enjoyed the gloat of survival, slithered into the brush behind me, and fled.

XI

I fled from my dead comrades as now I race to join the living. I did not ask to be a survivor, it had been thrust upon me. Back there are all my dead. Inert like broken trees after the storm has passed; like stones upon the beach, covered and uncovered as the heavy waves, like men, rise and fall, rise and fall. Soon I shall smile at my living comrades, again find my confraternity.

The bay is fleet, the sorrel on our lead gleams under a startling sun. I shall give him to Tupac as a gift to seal our comradeship. The victory here will be Tupac's and then, my self-imposed exile having already endured too long, I shall return to my homeland where the victories —and defeats—will be my own.

We gallop through the ichu grass, pass a huge bear who, having strayed from the forest, stops to stare. We scatter several vicuña who have wandered from their herd. Enter the forest which stands athwart the puna. It is thick with trees and heavy brush. The sun is lost. Gone are east and west, south and north. I stop for fear we will go in circles. Fire a burst. Receive my response and turn the bay in its direction. I coax her into a walk and she singlesteps with delicate beauty. We go among the mahogany, the tall jacaranda, the colo, the black walnut, enter into a great stand of cedar. A peccary scuttles and hides. Overhead a sloth sleeps. A boa constrictor, its malevolent head swiveling from atop its long, sturdy turret, eyes us with cold disdain. The fragrant scent, the cool green shade, the mighty boughs, the cedars' fine interlacing foliage all conspire to give me sweet solace. Not for the dead but for the living. The dead are dead and soon forgot, for the tears remembered are too heavy for our slight shoulders. We exist only because we can forget—and *beg*et. I laugh. Oh, there they are. I hear their voices, the metallic clang of arms; soon their fraternal eyes will look upon me, search me out, probe my flesh like burning fagot ends.

The sorrel yanks his lead from my hands; the bay mare rears under me, whinnies, refuses to go forward on my urging. "Move on," I say, "they are friends." She sidesteps, turns her head, rears, her eyes wild with fright. She has seen or smelled what I have not yet seen or smelled. As she rears again, I leap from the saddle. Speak to her and the sorrel softly, tether them, proceed on foot. Make a few turnings among the trees.

Enter into a small clearing. Stand transfixed. For there is Theo, tongue protruding from his gaunt tormented face, hanging from a jacaranda. In death he has befouled himself and the stench clings to him as if to hide from the million red ants which feed on it and him.

There is no time for mourning. I merely climb the tree and cut him down, cover him with a blanket. At least let the red ants feed in darkness.

Now I know. I step around the few remaining trees

and there before my feverish eyes lies the shallow bowl, the bloodstained arena, its heaps of slag gardening my hopes, my dreams, my fraternal dead. I scream and wheel to find my horses, but they are gone.

I hear a barked command. "Do not kill him!"

My gun leaps, bursts, enflames the countryside.

Too late.

I feel a searing pain, and fall. Ramón Cordes has lost the day.

XII

Caged at last.

I lie staring at the roughly cut beams that support the unevenly planed boards that are the ceiling and roof of the room and hut. The door to the room is bolted from the outside of course. Whenever someone prepares to enter I can hear the squeak and clank of the sliding bolt. I advised them that lacking oil a little piss will remedy its rusty resistance. They neither smiled nor paid me heed.

I lie on the bed fully clothed. The fever is gone. I feel better. They have cut away a trouser leg the easier to cleanse and bind the wound in my leg. The pain is slight. I enjoy my rest.

Thus far they have treated me well. Did so even when I had fought like a wild beast, clawed at their eyes, bit into their flesh when they took me captive. Still I sneer at them because I know they treat me well only because they are intimidated by those who are leaders, rulers, commanders, survivors. I in their stead would show no mercy.

When they ushered in the photographer I almost

115

laughed in their faces. He carried a large North American Polaroid camera and took several shots of me from different angles. I smiled for the camera. When the last had been developed, they were shown to me. I turned my head away. I take no comfort in viewing my own face. It reminds me of the charming days of my childhood, the faces of my old ones, of my brothers and sisters, of the downcast muted eyes of those who served us.

After they bolted the door behind them I roared with laughter. They would send my photographs north, out of the country, to ascertain my identity. They could not quite believe they had taken the great, the elusive, the legendary Ramón Cordes.

They had asked my name but I had refused to answer. It is a game I play to gain little victories. I pile one on the other to construct a haphazard wall before my eyes to conceal the major defeats.

Why not? I suffer. They have me caged. Have hammered heavy planking to the windows, permitting only enough space between the boards for air and splintery slivers of sun to enter. I am certain the guard around the hut is numerous and heavily armed. Perhaps they believe the benevolent Lord will lay hands upon me and I shall rise to demolish the temple of my imprisonment. Or the peasants and miners will storm the hut to free me. Or my loyal friend will arrive with an army. Or my dead will rise. Perhaps Simone will descend from the heavens with her cannons bare, firing sour milk shells. Or revolutionary students will liquidate their inheritances, launch an armada, sail across the galloping seas, storm the coastal bastions and rescue Ramón Cordes from these grubby little beasts who have at last snared him—the ferocious warbler. The inept sloth. Yes, now

116

that it is about to terminate, I can admit the venture has been inept, slothful, ludicrous, sentimental, self-defeating from its very inception. Humiliating.

Only death will redeem me.

Will they be idiotic enough—yes, they will, I wager it—to shoot me now? Their prisoner? Wounded? A perfect *mise en scène* for martyrdom and redemption. It is the sort of error they always commit—it is not that they are stupid, that is a conceit manufactured by fools and children: if stupid, how is it they have ruled the earth for three thousand years?

Shot, the revolution will cannibalize my flesh, grow fat on it; caged, I will become a *cause célèbre*, a rallying point. Given my freedom, I will have no place to go—will not even be welcome on the *rive gauche*. I will be finished, will disappear for the last time, become lost in the crowd like an ex-cinema idol grown fat and old, cadging drinks from strangers.

No, they will not give me my freedom, that would take more courage and imagination than they are known to possess. And I? I would not have the courage to take my freedom if given. I would plunge the barrel of a gun into my mouth and shoot my mediocre head to bony bits and slimy pieces. When a man is of no further use, and knows it, he ought to deprive himself of life.

I am spending too much time with this. There is no need for concern. They will do the nasty job for me. And quickly, too!

And I will sprout gossamer wings and fly off to heaven, my kindly soul pink and hairy. I have called myself cruel. Compared to Marguerite and Rojos I am a bubbly little angel, pissing a white, sweet wine. And Marguerite and Rojos? They piss piss.

The whores.

Oh, my God!

My heart begins to pound, blood to rush to my head too quickly, my wounded leg to throb, to fever, burn, my arms to thresh about, my lungs to choke, the walls are falling in on me so that I throw my hands out wildly to save myself from being crushed to death. I can feel immense sobs rushing to break loose from the profound depths of myself. No, no, I must not wail, must not give way to that suppressed howl which I have so long contained in my vast solitude. They will hear me and snicker—not yet, no, I am not yet defeated, not until all breath has ceased.

Is this how it is all to end?

I must not think of Marguerite and Rojos. They are out of it. It rests between me and my captives, and I must concentrate on dying bravely so my very last moment will be decorated with the pennants of honor. Honor? For one such as I? A childish charade as ancient as human life. Or is it only the cover for an older, more vicious game? Man—no, not man, I—I am so fond of embroidering my mask with junk finery, colored glass beads. To face death bravely means to make my departure with the sweetest smile in all of life scribed on my lips for eternity—the smile of victory. They will understand then that frail though I had been, deceived as I had been, Ramón Cordes had not been defeated.

Calm again, I readjust the folded blanket which is my pillow under my head. With my fingers I comb the hair which frames my face. Lean, handsome face. At least that is what I have been told. I dislike mirrors and through the years have avoided sight of my reflection. But women have told me they loved me because I was handsome. Others because I was cruel. Some even be-

118

cause I was tender. Many because through me they tasted the revolution. Salted, bitter, alive. One, a Congolese with a flat nose and thick, thirsty lips, her eyes large, round, as soft as a bay mare's, told me she loved me because she feared me—that I was enamored with death. To defeat me, she said, was to defeat death. I laughed. Did not believe her. Shunted her aside.

I wander. Cast my eyes about what I am certain will be my last battlefield. Freshly calcimined, its lime-white pleases me. A clean, austere purity. In addition to the bed upon which I now lie, there are the roughly made wood table and chair in a corner of the room. It is between the bed and the chair that I now journey, my circumscribed life. That is all. The sole ornamentation are the abstract murals the sun vagariously designs in accordance with the earth's orbit as it slants vertically through the cracks left by the up and down boards that bar the two windows. On the table a desiccated yellow candle flickers as it stands in a tallow-encrusted tin dish. My right hand, as though completely independent of the body, gropes for words. Reflex. The habit of a lifetime —or at least since the day I joined Markos more than twenty years ago. "The single way that I must go"—a line cribbed from a letter Rilke once wrote to a young poet—had been the very first entry. Yes, I began my career as a revolutionary with a heresy. Intended always to strike it from the journal, rip out the page, but never did. Instead I pretended to myself I had forgotten its presence—a few words, a phrase, a secret mark that over the subsequent years I wandered from, lost, forgot, betrayed, but to which I somehow, unwillingly, always returned.

It is to me a cruel, a terrifying line. An implacable

demand. And I made it of myself, not comprehending that I could not be as patient as I believed myself to be (I, the most impatient of men) towards all—again I imprecisely rob Rilke of his words—"towards all that is unsolved in my heart for the questions themselves are like locked rooms and like books written in an exotic tongue."

So I have failed, betrayed my secret mark, and have become a man who approaches his end from a totally unforeseen direction—suffering nails in his flesh, and martyrdom in his eyes. Again less—or more—than human.

Soon the entire world will know of my fiasco, for my defeat on the field has been complete: my personal papers, correspondence, campaign notebooks and diaries have been captured by the enemy. A catastrophe. The world press will publish the history attested to in my own hand of my every act, error, thought and heresy. I blush now at each failure etched so boldly in my clear and graceful hand. My comrades, admirers—not friends, for friendships are antipathetic to the revolution—will shout "Forgery!" and make the accusation stick. They have expertise in performing such miracles. After the shouting has died, they will delete what they believe harmful to the cause, retrieve and publish the remainder as the unabridged and true journal of Ramón Cordes.

Some will cheer, others deride, men and women will genuflect before my graven image and kiss their thumbs, still others spit their phlegm.

And as always, they will miss the point.

What was—is—the point? What was it that drove me on? I can hardly say. Too much time has passed, too many battles. I thought I would become a wandering

120

revolutionary in the way men once became wandering minstrels—yet I was born in the twentieth century, came to adulthood in its second half. I was like a spirit who wandered in from the past and became immediately captured by the present—infused with blood, bones, flesh and a tortured, indecisive imagination. I was held in chains, thought I was free, knew I was not. Now when I glance over my shoulder, all I can see is a vast junk heap piled high with the debris of history: corpses, exploded houses, the unraveling corners of tattered black and red banners flapping listlessly from under blackened stones. I strummed my lute and blood spouted from men's eyes.

I tried to stop, to consider, could not. Saw my eyes reflected in a window glass. Shattered it, passed on. Propelled forward by the sheer weight of fear: if I fell to my knees, I should never again find the energy necessary to rise.

A bad reason, but there it is. A depressing letdown for my comrades and admirers, for those who are already writing the eulogies.

In the past, it is true, a few tried to read me, but I held them off. What business was it of theirs? My inner life was my own, I gave them enough—more, all of the rest. My trade is—was—revolution. It was not my doing that I was mythicized, fantasized, elevated to television and cinema stardom. I was a quiet man who lived by his trade, my self concealed so I could wander about the earth at will, unknown, unnoticed. I had no desire to be made plastic, since I considered myself authentic. I dealt with reality arrived at via cold logic: before one could remake the world it would of course be necessary to tear it down. One sought allies among the deracinated, the déclassé, the dispossessed, not for reasons of justice but for the very human reason—whether good or evil I cannot say—that they were one's own. Selfish, I know.

To believe otherwise is to believe that one is—again—less or more than human. It is then the atrocities begin. The enemy's, mine. I am pocked with eyes like running sores.

Those very men who rebel not because of empathy with the impoverished but because they find the world they are part of fake, plastic as they term it, have themselves made plastic everything they touch with their fat, greedy fingers. Including me, Ramón Cordes. They have taken me, who has spent my years in the shadows, in the alleyways, in the mountains and canebrakes, who has avoided the cameras, the klieg lights, the newsreels, who has been satisfied to allow others the glory and the weapons of power, who has avoided any glass from which I could see my own reflection, and they have placed my face—more than life-size—on a million posters and nailed them to a million walls. (Does the deed follow the wish?) For the world to see what I myself have never wished to see. When I came upon one of those portraits of myself in the house of a friend, above the sofa, the wall of honor, illumined by a powerful spot, I shuddered from shame and dread.

Was that Ramón Cordes? That face of pure innocence made rakish by that jaunty guerrilla fatigue cap from under the bill of which shone two intensely black, very insane eyes? CORDES!

Shame and dread (I knew then I was already dead) followed by a terrifying ennui. I coughed, spat blood, begged my friend's pardon, and left. Correction: no longer friend. He had joined the conspiracy to make me less than human. Or more. Equal. That is, more or less are equal for the result is the same. Not human.

In that way is a man's life diminished. In what sense can a man be said to be victorious over nature or history if he is either superhuman or plastic? By hanging my poster portrait over his sofa my erstwhile friend had both elevated himself and lessened me. Is it for that that I have dared to outstare those bloodshot eyes which torment me day and night? At another time I would have put a bullet through his head!

See! That is what I have become.

Yes, it can be said I am harsh, perhaps cruel. It is certain that I am obsessed, driven. Tools of my trade.

Am? Was. I become confused. Cannot make my escape. The sun no longer paints murals on the wall. The candlelight has flickered out. *I am caged! Less than a man and more than a beast!* When all I ever wanted was simply to be human.

I close my eyes and search for sleep.

XIII

The sleeping soldier, his carbine between his knees, his back against the batten door, was roused by the overhead roar of a motor, the whirr of propellers. A helicopter, a whirlybird. He jumped to his feet and stood alertly athwart the threshold.

In a few minutes the generals appeared, polished. He saluted sharply and they responded in kind. He threw the rusty bolt, flung open the door, and carbine in hand, led the way into the prisoner's room. Put struck match to candle. The captive's cage flamed into quavery yellow light. The prisoner, who had been sleeping, opened his eyes, acknowledged his visitors with a calm smile, and sat up, back to the wall.

The soldier wondered at the man's easy authority. It was so strong the soldier thought he could actually see the authority of the two generals pass into the man, who expanded from it, as the generals diminished. Was it the quavering candlelight which bemused his eyes? Was it really true that the generals, sturdy, strong, harsh, stood before the captive as he himself always stood before them? Afraid, abject? It could hardly be true. The two generals were renowned for their bravery and cruelty. But the soldier had to admit that their reputation suffered in comparison to that of the man sitting so calmly on the cot—only his black, intense eyes windowing his own cruelty and courage.

The generals, serious of mien, compared photographs, examined the man. Looked at one another, nodded.

One spoke, the senior officer. "You could have saved us the trouble. You are Cordes."

Cordes shrugged, but said nothing.

Again the general spoke. "Is there anything at all you wish to say?"

Cordes eyed him with a thin, arrogant smile, coldly. "It is all in that little notebook. If you give it to me I'll sign it."

The senior officer signaled to the soldier, who picked up the notebook from the table and handed it to the general, who in turn passed it on to Cordes.

"This is my confession, my passion, my agony. You will misread it—as will my comrades. That is inevitable. But it contains what I would have said had I spoken. There is now nothing more to say." Given a pen, he wrote his name on the last page. "I have initialed each leaf. I would like nothing altered—I want my epigraph and epitaph to be unified and one. The sooner, the kinder."

The generals smiled. The second said, "You are of our class."

Cordes raised a black eyebrow, gazed at the generals contemptuously. "I am of the soldier's class." Then in the voice of command, "No more now."

Inwardly the soldier smiled, for the captive's tone was

one of dismissal, he commanded here, and strangely the generals obeyed. They wheeled sharply and left the room, followed by the soldier.

After the soldier had bolted the door, the senior officer issued his instructions, unsheathed and handed him the pistol from his holster, saluted, and both departed.

The soldier, after they had left, observed his captive through the crack in the batten door. Cordes still sat calmly, staring into space. He looked amused.

The helicopter's engine coughed, roared into life, the propellers whirred. As it passed directly overhead the hut shook, and then it was gone. Soon thereafter the soldier heard horses being saddled, mounted, then gallop off.

The adobe hut was now empty but for the soldier and his prisoner.

Over the mine camp the gray sky of dawn began to shimmer with the gold and magenta rays of the sun ascending far to the east, beyond the valley. The mine camp was devoid of human life. The open shaft loomed ominously black in the mountainside. The rickety barracks leaned in sharp outline, desolate and precarious on its rotted timbers. The iron donkeys, encrusted with slag, stood poised on the narrow rails, their rust reflecting a dull blood-red sheen from the fires beginning now to enflame the still cold gray-blue furnace which was the sky. The slag heaps looked like piles of ash from a burnt-out earth. Tethered to the old wrecked jeep, under which a young guerrilla had sought protection and found death, was a horse. The soldier's.

He stood before the batten door, guarding Cordes. Inside the room, the captive still sat, beguiled by his thoughts.

126

As dawn encroached on day, the soldier heard a whistle from the hills beyond the mine clearing. He nodded assent, he would do as commanded. Still, the man was a killer—and killers should be killed. That was the law of the land, of his ancestors, handed down from generation to generation over the centuries. Very few ever broke that law—and if they did they were marked as fools or saints. He was neither.

A command was a command. The signal had been given.

He slid the bolt and entered the small darkened room. The candle had long before sputtered, then died. The captive's lean face was impaled with darting sharp splinters of red and yellow light. The soldier, his uniform ill-fitting, his shoulders slack, shuffled to the captive's side, the pistol heavy in his hand.

Cordes sighed, smiled sadly, warmed his hands at his lips. "It's the killing hour, I suppose. You seem afraid. Am I to be your first atrocity?"

The soldier lowered his eyes, said nothing.

"Don't be afraid. Do it quickly. I promise not to haunt you."

The soldier bit his nether lip, shrugged a heavy shoulder, turned, laid the pistol gently on the table, and without looking back, departed.

As he mounted his horse, he heard the captive's harsh cry, "Don't mock me! I am Ramón Cordes!"

"The majority of men are very proud of their constancy, of the steadfastness of their plans. They are as consistent as the steel in a broken or rusted compass. They know where they are going, and where they came from. Each stop along the way of life has already been counted and calculated.

"If we listen to them they will tell us: 'Let's not dally to look at the stars or the sea: it's best not to get distracted. The road is waiting. We run the risk of not getting to the end.'

"The end! What an illusion! There is no end in life. The end is a point in space and time, and no more transcendental than the point that preceded or follows."

—Pío Baroja